kate GORDON GREW UP IN a VERY BOOKY HOUSE, WITH two librarian parents, in a small town by the sea on the north-west coast of Tasmania.

In 2009, Kate was the recipient of a Varuna writer's fellowship. Her first book, *Three Things About Daisy Blue* – a young adult novel about travel, love, self-acceptance and letting go – was published in the Girlfriend series by Allen & Unwin in 2010.

Now Kate lives with her husband and her very strange cat, Mephy Danger Gordon. Every morning, while Kate writes, Mephy Danger sits behind her on the couch with his tail curled around her neck.

Kate was the recipient of a 2011 Arts Tasmania Assistance to Individuals grant, which means she can now spend more time losing herself in the world of Thylas and Sarcos. She is currently working on the sequel to *Thyla*.

Kate blogs at **www.kategordon.com.au/blog** and you can follow her on Twitter at **www.twitter.com/misscackle**. She sometimes says some funny stuff!

thyla

kate gordon

RANDOM HOUSE AUSTRALIA

A Random House book
Published by Random House Australia Pty Ltd
Level 3, 100 Pacific Highway, North Sydney NSW 2060
www.randomhouse.com.au

First published by Random House Australia in 2011

Addresses for companies within the Random House Group can be found at
www.randomhouse.com.au/offices.

National Library of Australia
Cataloguing-in-Publication Entry

Author: Gordon, Kate, 1982–
Title: Thyla / Kate Gordon
ISBN: 978 1 86471 881 2 (pbk.)
Notes: For young adults
Subjects: Tasmania – Juvenile fiction
Dewey number: A823.4

Cover photographs courtesy Getty Images
Cover design by Christabella Designs
Internal design by Christabella Designs
Typeset in Minion 11/17 pt by Midland Typesetters, Australia
Printed in Australia by Griffin Press, an accredited ISO AS/NZS 14001:2004
Environmental Management System printer

10 9 8 7 6 5 4 3 2 1

The paper this book is printed on is certified against the
Forest Stewardship Council® Standards. Griffin Press holds
FSC chain of custody certification SGS-COC-005088. FSC
promotes environmentally responsible, socially beneficial
and economically viable management of the world's forests.

For my mum, who is my real-life Connolly. For my dad, who wrote the first story about a tiger called Tessa. For Dad's Leigh, for painting the picture that inspired the story. For Tasmania, for its rich history. And for my Leigh, for everything.

CHAPTER

ONE

my name is tessa.

It was the one thing I knew for certain, the one word that stood lonely in my head when the lights were turned on.

The lights were so bright they were like darkness. My eyes watered. It felt as though they were bleeding.

I opened my mouth, and what I wanted to be a scream came out as a whimper. It sounded foreign and I felt myself thinking, *I don't whimper.*

And so that was the second thing I knew.

Beyond that, there was nothingness.

Hot tears tumbled down my face and I wanted to push them back in.

I don't cry, either.

I was warm. Too warm. I could feel something bearing down on me – at once soft and horribly heavy – and another word joined *Tessa* in my mind, as if the words were small creatures meeting together.

Blankets.

And then, *I don't like blankets.*

And so now I knew four things.

But the rest was deafening emptiness.

I didn't know where I was.

I didn't know how I got there.

I didn't know *who* I was, beyond my name, and that I didn't like blankets.

I didn't know who the other people in the room were. They hadn't spoken yet, but I knew they were there. I could smell them. I could hear their shallow breathing. I could feel their fear.

Somehow this comforted me.

They are scared too, I thought. I fought through the pain, and I opened my eyes wide again and sat up.

'Who am I?' I asked.

And the woman screamed.

CHapteR

two

WE LAUGH ABOUT IT NOW, CONNOLLY.

How you were afraid of me at first, when now we are closer than many real mothers and daughters. You ask if I can blame you.

I can't.

When you showed me a mirror that first day, I screamed too. You think that's funny now, also.

I did look a fright.

My hair – now cropped short like a boy's – was long and clumped into pudgy, misshapen sausages.

My face was so thick with dirt you could not tell the colour of my skin.

My eyes were red and bloodshot, and my lips were cracked and torn. My body was one big bruise.

I was a monster.

I don't blame Vinnie for instructing you gruffly, 'Wash her. Make her look human.'

Vinnie is your overseer. He has a deep, growling voice and a face that forever looks vexed. His cologne is always too strong – it smells of spice and whiskey. His hair is greying about the temples, but aside from this he looks younger than you would expect in someone of such rank. He is thickset and strong-jawed and he has eyes of the most intriguing colour – a sort of amber, with golden flecks. And, though I know it must sound odd, I felt I knew those eyes. But my brain was befuddled. If Vinnie knew me, he would tell me.

My memories of those first days with you and Vinnie are blurred and smudged. They seem to me like paintings with the paint still wet. I feel I can push my fingers into them and mix the colours up, or wipe them away completely.

You helped me to make things more solid, Connolly.

'These things take time, Tessa,' you said, when I asked you why Vinnie's search – for my parents, for my history, for *anything* about me – was uncovering nothing. 'Vinnie is a really great policeman. He'll find something. Until then, well, you've got me!'

I appreciated – I *still* appreciate – how you strove to make me feel safe. You were a police officer, not a governess. You did not know me, really. You didn't *have* to visit me in hospital, spend time with me; comfort me.

You asked me, on perhaps the third or fourth day, if I had any sense of who I was as a person; whether I was a kind person. I think you were trying to make me feel better, weren't you? You were trying to make me say that I felt I was good and virtuous.

But the thing is, Connolly, that's not how I felt at all. I felt I had *tried* to be good. I felt like I had tried to right wrongs. But I felt like I had failed. What wrongs they were, and how I failed, I couldn't remember.

'I feel as if I need a purpose,' I said. 'A purpose outside of myself. Something to take my mind off . . .'

Off what?

I couldn't *remember.*

This is what I *do* remember:

The hunger. No matter how much you fed me, it wasn't enough. I could have eaten ten more plates at every meal.

'Gawd, Tess. Where do you put it all?' you said, laughing, as I gobbled up the meal of pancakes and syrup you brought me from a place you called 'Maccas'. You'd had to smuggle it past the nursing staff, who seemed to believe very highly in the benefits of fruit, jelly and pasty white bread that didn't taste like bread at all. 'I'd turn into a complete lardarse if I ate like you do.'

'Lardarse?' I asked, through a mouthful of pancake, so it came out more like 'lar-ar?'.

'Fat,' you said. You were used, by now, to me not understanding some of your words.

The thought of getting fat scared me a little bit. I didn't want to be fat. I suspected that it would make me slow. It would make me *weak*. I didn't want to be weak.

I left half of my last pancake on my plate. Then I stared at it for a while. Then I gobbled it up.

Vinnie came to visit me too, but he did not bring pancakes. Instead, he brought his gruff voice and his glare and his coffee-stained suit.

And questions. He brought with him so many questions.

'I've had no luck locating your parents,' he said, never looking up from the clipboard he held on his knee. 'It's pretty hard when you don't have a name. You really can't remember any name? First or last? Of anyone?'

I shook my head. Vinnie sighed. 'I've been talking to Social Services about your case,' he said, and I was too afraid to ask what 'Social Services' was. It sounded like a company that might be responsible for balls and dancing.

I hoped not. I didn't believe I would be a very good dancer.

While I thought, horrified, of waltzes and quadrilles (and where those names came from, no, I did not know),

Vinnie spoke some more. Words drifted into my ears and even though I knew their meaning, my head felt fuzzy – the words seemed formless. I was too distracted and fearful to make sense of them. 'Guardian', 'school', 'place to live'. I hoped I could ask you, later, to explain.

As Vinnie left – without ever once having looked me in the face (I wondered if this was some strange, nervous habit. But Vinnie didn't *seem* nervous), he turned and said, 'So you really don't remember *anything*. Nothing at all?'

'No,' I whispered. 'Nothing at all.'

The doctors confirmed I had lost my memory, due probably to a head injury when I fell in the bushland, though any outward signs of this injury had disappeared. They presented this fact to me as though it were a revelation.

'Perhaps I should be a doctor,' I whispered to you. 'I made the diagnosis far more quickly than they did.'

You growled at me for being 'cheeky'. But as you said it you swallowed a smile.

The doctors commented on the fast healing of my injuries. They said they had hardly needed to treat me after that first day. They only kept me in hospital because of my lost memory.

And because of the scars.

The doctors did not yet have a diagnosis for them – the markings on my back. The long, thin, striping slashes. They asked me if I remembered how or when they appeared. I just stared at them. Did they really expect me to say it again?

'I. Don't. Remember,' I said finally, through gritted teeth.

When you and Vinnie weren't there, and the doctors were away attending other patients, the days were composed of long stretches of dull, interminable nothing. I hated being confined to the bed. I hated being in the stark white room with its unnatural smells. I hated the 'television' you were so excited to see. I did not know how to make it work, and I was *glad*. When you turned it on, it seemed like witchcraft and at first I was slightly afraid of it. 'It's like moving camera obscura,' I whispered to you, and your brow furrowed for a moment.

'How can you have never seen a TV?' you asked. Then, when you saw I was becoming more and more distressed by the tiny people cavorting in the small black box, you said, 'It's nothing to be scared of, Tess. You're right. It's just moving photographs. It's pretty boring, actually.'

Soon, once the fear and then the novelty subsided, I found I agreed with you. The 'programmes' were boring, the 'presenters' insufferable, and as for the 'actors', well, they didn't even look like real human beings! Their faces were tight and shiny and barely moved. And many of them were an unnatural orange hue that disturbed me.

They looked like they had been rubbing themselves with marmalade. I was glad you didn't pressure me to use the television. Instead, you brought me books, which I liked, but even these I tired of. I longed to be *up* and *out*.

The other thing I remember from these hospital days is constant, unrelenting fear. Fear of the not-knowing, certainly, but also, strangely, fear of the *knowing*. I had nightmares – awful, shadowy nightmares – of darkness and screaming and blood. There was little detail, just shadows and slashes of red, and yet the dreams terrified me. Whenever I closed my eyes these dark dreams came to me. They seemed like memories and I thought, *If these are memories, perhaps I do not want to remember.* I did not tell you about these nightmares. I didn't want to worry you.

I did tell you, however, that there was a part of me that was fearful of finding out my past.

'I think you know the most important thing,' you said to me, holding a freckled hand against my cheek. 'You know you like to help people. You know you need a purpose. You know you are giving. Remember the little boy?'

I did remember him. It had happened only the day before. A young boy – perhaps only three years old – had wandered, lost and alone, into my hospital room.

'Hello,' I said. 'Who are you, then, young man?'

'Jordan,' he replied in a whisper. 'Jordan John Possum.'

'And where are your parents?' I asked.

'I don't know,' Jordan said, his chin wobbling.

'Me neither,' I said, pushing myself up from the bed. It still hurt to do so, but I knew it was no time to be a coward. The boy needed me. 'All right, Jordan. Let us find them,' I said.

You discovered me walking around the hospital holding Jordan's hand in mine, knocking on doors and asking for a Mr and Mrs Possum.

We found Jordan's parents – the Hopes, not the Possums – in the reception area, asking frantically for help to find their son.

'Possum!' Jordan's mother cried. 'Where have you been?'

'I've been with Tessa,' he said. 'It's okay. She made me safe.'

The woman looked up at me with her grey-blue eyes. I could tell she thought that I – the wild, unkempt creature that I was – did not seem the type to worry about the safety of a child. Still, she nodded. 'Thank you,' she said, and then held out her hand. 'I'm Chloe,' she said. 'This is Daniel. Thank you, Tessa, for what you did.'

'I *needed* him to be safe,' I told you later. 'Like you make me safe.'

'I'll always make sure you're safe, Tessa,' you said, your voice very serious. 'No matter what happens, we will be friends. I'll always be there for you.'

I didn't ask you why you visited me so much more often than Vinnie did. I didn't ask why you stroked my hair as the doctors examined me or why you held my hand while they poked and prodded and jabbed at me. I didn't ask why you spent hours consoling me after the nurse cut off my hair (and consoling *them* over the bite I gave them while they were doing so).

I worried that, if I asked you why you were doing it, you might not be able to think up a good enough reason.

And you might leave me.

And I wanted so badly to stay with you. I felt safe with you. When I was with you, the nightmares were held at bay and the bad memories could not touch me. I felt like I was in the light.

It was like having a mother. You stroked my newly stubbled hair. You even read to me when I was too tired to lift the book. You read me *White Fang*. I liked the wolves. I hated the men.

You visited after work and sometimes in your lunch break, because the police station was not far away.

And then you brought me my notebook.

'It's for writing down your memories when they come back,' you said. 'It's to help you piece together the puzzle.

You can write in it every night or whenever you have a quiet moment. You can write down everything.'

'But can't I just tell you?' I asked. 'That's what I've *been* doing.'

And I had. I had been telling you every single time something little came back to me. I had a little assembly now, a little team of memories:

- Tessa (my name)
- scars (still there, still hurting, still confusing the doctors. 'They seem unnatural,' I heard one young doctor say. 'Inhuman.' I did not let that doctor look at me again.)
- blankets (I did not like them)
- meat (I did like it, very much)
- sandwiches (not so much)
- walls (I did *not* like them. I wanted to *jump* them)
- trousers (I liked wearing them and hated wearing skirts, even though something inside me told me that I *should* prefer skirts)
- bright light (scary)
- darkness, when I was alone in my room (even *more* scary)
- and, finally:
- parents (gone. 'Dead?' 'I don't know.')

When I told you the last one, you looked at me with an expression that was curious and strange.

'What?' I asked, and you told me, 'Nothing,' and I wished, right then, and very hard, that I knew more about you. You knew absolutely everything that *I* knew about me, and I knew nothing about you. I didn't ask, though. I didn't want you to think that I was prying. I didn't want you to tire of me and leave me.

I was good, so good.

And still you abandoned me.

'The book is for when you leave here,' you said. 'For when you go to school.'

Chapter

three

THIS IS THE LAST PIECE WE REMEMBER TOGETHER BEFORE I started at Cascade Falls College. I'm sorry it isn't a nicer memory. I was angry. I didn't want you to leave me. Even so, I could have been nicer.

You drove me out to the school. I knew that it was not your job to do this, and I should have been grateful, but still I couldn't soothe the anger enough to speak even one word to you on the way there.

The journey took forty-five minutes instead of the ten minutes you told me it would. There were two reasons.

Firstly, the journey was by *car*. Now, I was sure I *had* been in a car before, though the word wasn't familiar. Certainly, when I saw the car, I recognised its shape, more or less. But when you asked me to get *in* the car, a heavy terror enveloped me. I didn't want to. The thought terrified me. I refused. I sat down on the side of the road and shook my head.

You said, 'But it's just a car, Tess. You've been in a car before, right?'

I buried my head in my arms. It was worse than the television. At least *other* people were stuck in the television, not me. It wasn't *right* to get in a metal box like that. It would move, but *how*? I wouldn't do it. You couldn't make me.

A low, rumbling growl escaped from my throat. I bared my teeth. I crouched down, close to the ground. *I would not go.*

But then, of course, after fifteen minutes of you stroking my hair and saying, 'It will be okay. Be brave. You're a brave girl, Tess. You can be brave about this', I got in. I *am* brave. So I got in. When the car moved, I screamed and clawed at the windows, but I settled down eventually into just being grumpy.

We also made a few detours on the way to Cascade Falls. You wanted to show me more of Hobart. Or maybe you didn't want to say goodbye yet.

When I had said goodbye to Vinnie, he'd just grunted, and looked anywhere but at me, as usual. He'd said, 'If we find anything out, we'll let you know. And if you remember *anything*, please let *me* know. It's important.'

He marched from the room.

I poked my tongue out at his back.

Vinnie made me mad. I wanted him to like me. I felt like he *should* like me, but I seemed to annoy him. I had never wanted to stick my tongue out at you. But that day, the day you left me, I felt you were just as bad as Vinnie. I felt you had never cared at all.

Thoughts were crashing about inside my head.

How dare you leave me? You're the only person I can trust! You're the only person I feel safe with! How could you be so mean? What will I do without you?

I will be so lonely at this school. I will be so afraid.

I couldn't remember ever having gone to school before, though you said I must have. I spoke well, and I knew about things like the camera obscura. I must have learned these things somewhere.

And, to be sure, I *did* remember some '*school*' things. I remembered wooden desks and pots of ink and long, pale uniform dresses, and chalk squeaking on blackboards, and a pinch-faced schoolmistress telling me to 'stand up straight', 'don't say "what", say "pardon".' When I told you this, you said it sounded like scenes from a historical movie. 'Schools aren't like that now,' you said.

I didn't ask you what a 'movie' was.

You told me all about Cascade Falls in the car while I simmered in grouchy silence. 'It's a good school, Tess.

You'll love it there. It's actually quite posh, but they have a good scholarship programme, and funding to help disadvantaged girls. There's a trust – the Lord Trust – that helps girls like you to go there. When the trustees found out about your situation, they were really eager for you to be a recipient. Oh, I just know you'll love it there, Tess.'

I didn't reply. You carried on, regardless. 'It's in a really nice setting and the main schoolrooms are in a huge, beautiful old sandstone building. I think maybe it was used once as offices for the Cascade Brewery – that's pretty much next door. When it was first built it was just that one building. Now there are some modern outbuildings, where they teach art and drama and a few other bits and pieces. There's a little courtyard in the middle of it all that I think you'll like. It would be nice to sit there, out in the sun.'

You stopped talking for a moment while you negotiated a large circular structure in the road. I looked out across the suburban streets, at the sunlight being drained away by the dark tar of the road. I wondered if there would be grass at Cascade Falls. I wondered if there would be trees. Sunlight on tar was nothing like sunlight dappling through the leaves of a tree.

'You're lucky to be going to Cascade Falls, Tess,' you said, once we had rounded the circle. 'I remember when I was a kid, at Taroona High, I always wished I could go to a posh private school like Cascade Falls. I used to see the girls in their straw boater hats and little white gloves and feel so envious of them. I thought life there must be really fun. I probably had that impression from reading one too many *Chalet School* books when I was younger. Although, of course, Cascade Falls isn't in the Austrian Alps. But it is halfway up a mountain!'

You told me I got into Cascade Falls because the school is one of only three in Hobart that still has boarding houses (and one of the others is Valley Grammar, which is an all-boys school), because of the Lord Trust, and because the headmistress, Ms Hindmarsh, is one of your closest friends.

'You'll love Cynthia,' you said. 'She's really friendly and funny and passionate. I've known her for years, from back in Campbell Town. We grew up there together – her and me and Raphael. That's . . . that *was* her husband. He's . . . gone now.' You were silent for a few moments, before shaking yourself and going on.

You asked me if I was nervous.

I humphed and looked out the window.

You asked me if I'd remembered to pack my new black stockings.

I rolled my eyes and started drumming my fingernails on the top of the car door.

Finally, you gave up asking me things, and started pointing out landmarks. I looked despite myself.

Everything was so foreign and new. Nothing at all looked familiar.

I played with the thought that maybe I was a refugee from another place – British India, perhaps, or the Americas – since it really did feel like I was in a foreign land.

But then I would look different, wouldn't I? And my accent would be different from yours and Vinnie's, but it is exactly the same (only sometimes you say different words from the ones I use).

The memories will come back, I told myself. That thought was at the same time comforting and terrible. After all, I wasn't entirely sure that I *wanted* the memories to come back. Not if they were full of darkness and screaming, like my dreams.

'That's the police headquarters,' you said, pointing at an ugly, box-like structure. 'That's where I work. Back that way is the botanic gardens, and the domain, and the cenotaph. I'll take you to the gardens soon. You'll like them. They're really pretty. Down that way is the river and the waterfront. My favourite restaurant, Mures, is there. I'll take you there one day. And just over that way is Salamanca. Hang on, I'll take a detour and show you a bit of it.'

You turned left and went down a long steep road, past high sandstone buildings, some of which did look *slightly* familiar. As if I had dreamed a version of this place that was almost the same, but not quite.

And then we came to 'Salamanca'.

And I *did* recognise this. Well, some it. The names of the inns and shops and bright signs and banners were all very unfamiliar. But the buildings themselves – again, it was like I had once dreamed some other version of them, but I definitely did recognise them.

'You like?' you asked. 'It's one of my favourite spots. Vinnie hates it. He reckons it's really commercialised and snooty. He prefers the Cascade Pub. I leave him to it. It's a bit rough up there for me. I mean, you see a few unsavoury types down here sometimes as well, but you get them all over, don't you? I'll take you here sometime, if you want. The Quarry is my favourite. They do really good chips.'

I just let Connolly talk as I watched the buildings whoosh by, feeling as if I was in a dreamland, partway between memory and the present.

It was the walls around Cascade Falls that I noticed first, before the building itself.

I don't like walls, I thought to myself.

And these walls were *very* bad ones.

They were tall – so tall that as we rounded the bend just before my new school, just past the grand stone building and rows of factory sheds that you told me was the brewery you had mentioned earlier, I couldn't see that it was there at all. All I could see was wall – yards and yards of yellow sandstone wall, like a big cardboard box placed in the middle of the wilderness.

Only this box had spikes – sharp and black – and I wondered, *Are they to keep people out? Or keep people in?*

I remembered the other building we had passed – the one you called the Female Factory. When you had said those words I felt a tightness in my chest, and my head whipped around, craning for a better glimpse at the square stone shape by the road.

I know that place, I thought. *I know that place.*

'It was a jail,' you explained. 'For female convicts. I went in there once. Never again. It gave me the shivers. So many ghosts.'

When I first saw the walls of Cascade Falls, I thought it looked more like a prison than the small square that was the Female Factory site. The Female Factory didn't have spiked walls. Perhaps they had had other methods of keeping their inmates inside.

You must have noticed my expression, because you said, 'I know, Tess. It looks a bit grim from outside the walls, but inside it's lovely. Trust me. And everybody is so nice. I wouldn't have sent Cat here if it wasn't a great school.'

'Cat?' I asked, before I could stop myself. I didn't *want* to ask it, but my mouth said the word all on its own, without my bidding.

'My daughter,' you said.

'Your daughter goes here?' I asked. 'You never told me that.'

It was meant as an accusation, a chastisement – another example of how nasty you were being to me.

And I'm sorry for that.

I didn't know.

You shook your head. 'No, Cat *went* here. She's not here now.'

'Where is she?'

When I look back at it now – at how bluntly I asked those questions, how unthinkingly and uncaringly – I shudder.

But, as I said, I didn't know.

I saw your eyes brim with tears, and I felt a lump rise in my own throat.

What had I said?

Why were you crying?

You stopped the car in a big open yard outside the walls, in the middle of many other cars. It made a crunching noise on the gravel that scared me a little bit. It sounded like thunder.

You turned to me. 'Cat's gone. Missing. That's why I moved here. I used to live in Campbell Town – I worked at the police station there – but after Cat went, I accepted a job here. I needed to be close to where she had been. She went missing on a bushwalk. It was a school bushwalk, but it wasn't the school's fault. Cat was always such a good girl when she lived with me in Campbell Town, but when she got to Cascade Falls . . . I guess she rebelled. She used to run away a lot. That's what she did that day. She just wandered off, even though Cynthia – Ms Hindmarsh – told her not to. She just disappeared into the bush.'

'Where in the bush?' I asked, but something inside me already knew the answer.

'Very near to where we found you,' you replied. 'In the Waterworks. Just near the mountain. Just over there, actually.'

I looked up towards the mountain and felt my body go cold. That was where I was found. I wondered if it was where I'd lived. It seemed so majestic and yet so forbidding. It would have been a glorious place to live, I thought, but a harsh one.

'I'll never forget that moment,' you said, your voice suddenly soft and tender. 'When I first saw you. Have I told you about that day?'

I shook my head. I knew what happened after you found me, but not what happened before.

'Well, we'd received an anonymous phone call, about a girl who'd been injured,' you explained. 'Vinnie and I went up there together and we saw you straight away. You were lying there in a pool of light; all lit up like a strange angel. In the car on the way there, I'd dared to hope it might be . . . but we found *you* instead. And I'm very glad to have found you!'

You put your hand on my shoulder as a new thought occurred to me. 'Is that why you've been so nice to me? Because of where I was found? Because you think I might have seen your daughter on the mountain?'

You shook your head. 'No. Well, maybe a bit, at first. But I've come to care about you a lot. Not because of Cat. Because of you. And, you know, once a mother, *always* a mother.'

I was not angry at you any more, Connolly. In those few seconds I stopped being angry and started feeling sad. And guilty.

'I'm sorry,' I began.

You clasped my arm with your freckled hand and said, 'No, Tess. It's okay. I know you're feeling hurt. And lost. And abandoned. And *I'm* sorry that I have to leave you. I would take you home with me – I really would – but it's against protocol. The other alternatives for you weren't really suitable – group homes and that sort of thing. After what you've been through, you need an adult to look out for you. At least I know that here Cynthia can keep an eye on you. As long as you let her. Don't fight her like Cat did, okay, Tess?'

I nodded and you went on. 'And she's set up the daughter of one of Vinnie's friends to look out for you, too. She'll be your peer mentor. Her name is Charlotte. I don't remember Cat talking about her, but then Cat didn't talk to me about anything much after she came here. Cynthia says she's a good girl, though. A prefect. I hope you'll like her.'

'Connolly?' I said.

'What, Tess?'

'If I remember anything about Cat, I'll tell you. I promise.'

And I meant it. Suddenly, strongly, I *needed* to find Cat. I needed to help you, to repay you. And I needed to make Cat safe. Some fuzzy memory whispered to me that I *could* do this. I *needed* to do this. Perhaps this was my purpose.

I now had a reason to *want* to remember. I had a reason to use this notebook.

'Thank you, Tessa,' you said. 'And I will never stop trying to find out who you are.'

cHapter
four

тнen you went and you Left me by myseLf.

You were going to come in with me and say hello to Cynthia but as I opened the car door, a call came through on the black box you called your 'two-way'. It was Vinnie. I recognised his voice, even with all the crackles and squeals.

'Connolly, are you done with the kid? I need you at the station.' It wasn't a request. I could tell that much.

'I'd better go,' you said, rolling your eyes. 'I'm sorry. Tell Cynthia we'll catch up for coffee soon. And call me. At least once a week. You have my phone number?'

I felt at the pocket of my new school skirt, the one you bought for me. Though I did not find the skirt agreeable – I found it uncomfortable compared with trousers, and I believed its length indecently short – I was thankful to you for buying it for me. I knew the other girls would be wearing similar skirts and I wished to look as they did. Inside the pocket, a piece of paper rustled: the piece of paper on which you had written your 'number'.

'Yes,' I said, and I decided I would work out later how exactly to use a 'phone'.

'Right, well, do. I mean it. I want to hear how you're going. And if ever you need me to come and visit, just let me know, okay? I live really close to here, just over in Sandy Bay, so I'm only ever a few minutes away.'

'I will,' I said. 'And thank you for . . . for your name. Thank you.'

I had no last name. None that I could remember, anyway, and so you had lent me yours, just until I remembered – or discovered – my own.

'Tessa Connolly,' you said. 'It has a nice ring to it.'

Then you held me close and whispered in my ear, 'Be brave, Tess. But please, be conscious, too. Be mindful. Look after yourself. And write in your book, okay?'

I promised I would. 'Every day.'

'Good girl,' you said, and patted my hair.

As you turned to get back in the car, I saw the sun sparkle on the tears in your eyes. It made you look as if you were lit from within. Like your soul was glowing.

I waved at you as your car went backwards out onto the road. You really are so clever to make your car work. It does look very complicated.

I wondered, suddenly, if I would ever drive a car. I supposed I would but, right then, the thought terrified me.

'First things first,' I said to myself as I walked towards the high metal gate that cut through the wall of Cascade Falls.

I took a deep breath, and pushed.

CHAPTER
five

'IT'S OKAY, TESS. YOU WEREN'T TO KNOW ABOUT THE intercom,' said Ms Hindmarsh as we walked towards the big building that hid behind the gate.

I was so embarrassed I couldn't even look up from the ground.

Intercom.

Another word I did not know the meaning of only five minutes ago. Five minutes ago, when the heavy gate would not budge no matter how hard I pushed, and I rattled on its bars and yelled at the top of my voice, 'Hello? Cynthia? Ms Hindmarsh? It's me, Tessa. I'm here!'

I really *wished* I had known the word 'intercom' when, a couple of minutes later, Ms Hindmarsh appeared at the gate with a burly man in green overalls, who was saying

to her, 'There she is, Cynthia. I told you she was a loony!
You want me to call the cops?'

'Actually, Bernard, I think it might have been the
police who brought her here. Well, one particular police
officer anyway. Am I right, Tessa?'

I nodded. 'I didn't know how to get in,' I mumbled,
feeling embarrassed already. Why had that man said I was
a loony? I only wanted to get inside. That didn't make
me a loony!

'Why didn't you just press the button?' asked
Bernard.

'I didn't see a . . . '

I glanced to one side and saw a big black box with
a green button in its middle and the words 'Push
to talk'.

'That button?' I asked. 'But I already *was* talking. I was
yelling! I didn't need a button for talking. I needed one for
getting inside the wall.'

Bernard snorted, his face turning pink. 'Is she serious?'
he asked.

'Bernard, thank you,' said Ms Hindmarsh. 'You can go
now. I'll take it from here.'

Apparently the button is something like a 'two-way'. If
you press it, it lets you talk to Ms Hindmarsh's secretary,
Miss Bloom, even though she is miles away inside the
walls of Cascade Falls. If she decides that you should be

allowed to enter, she presses a button on *her* side, and the gate magically opens.

I really don't remember seeing anything like an intercom button before. I felt, not for the first time, as though I had woken up in an HG Wells novel.

Ms Hindmarsh was very nice about it, but I felt silly anyway.

It took me a good couple of minutes before I felt my embarrassment fade just enough that I could look up at Ms Hindmarsh. She was very pretty and young and had curly blonde hair and a very small nose with freckles on it. Not as many freckles as you have, Connolly, and they are smaller. Kind of like a fine sprinkling of dark pollen across her nose. Her face was happy and kind, and I immediately felt I might like her, especially because I knew she was your friend.

And then, after I looked at her and she smiled, I looked up at my new school.

What I saw made me stop very still and catch my breath.

It really was lovely.

You were right, Connolly. Cascade Falls is very pretty indeed!

There are trees and there is grass, which made me glad. And the building itself was not as horrid to me as the other intimidating boxes we had passed. It seemed welcoming, and its shape seemed, to me, like the way buildings *should* be shaped.

It is not a *very* large building. More medium-sized. It is a bit bigger than the Church of St David's that you showed me in the city, but smaller than the art gallery.

Its roof is pointed in three places, and in each of the points there is a lovely stained glass panel, with pictures of angels and birds and animals. Tasmanian animals. I saw a possum and a wallaby and on the largest panel – the centre one – there was a Tasmanian devil and a Tasmanian tiger. I was proud to remember all of the names of the animals, and I thought the last ones – the devil and tiger – were especially captivating. I looked at the sun gleaming on the glass, and I felt my belly ache with longing.

I did not know what it was, but I longed for *something* just outside of memory and the dull pain of it vibrated around my body.

I shook my head. I willed tears away. *I do not cry.*

'Do you like our stained glass?' asked Ms Hindmarsh.

'It's lovely,' I replied.

'Thank you,' she said, smiling. 'My husband's great-great-great-grandfather started it, way back in the 1830s, and my husband finished it a few years ago.'

Ms Hindmarsh suddenly looked as though she was in pain. I remembered what you had told me about

Ms Hindmarsh's husband being 'gone'. I tried to make her feel better.

'He was very talented,' I said.

'Yes, he is,' said Ms Hindmarsh. I opened my mouth to say something about what you had told me – about Raphael being gone. Why had Ms Hindmarsh said 'is', as though he was still alive? But Ms Hindmarsh looked so sad, Connolly. I knew it would be wrong of me to ask. Perhaps it hurt her too much to think of him as gone.

'I only hope you like the rest of Cascade Falls just as much as you like this,' she went on, wrenching her eyes away from the stained glass. Her voice was brighter now. 'Has Rachel told you much about the school?'

'Rachel?' For a moment, the name was foreign to me, and then I remembered. 'Connolly?'

'She's always Rachel to me,' Ms Hindmarsh said, smiling. 'Occasionally, she's even "Rachie", but don't tell her I told you that. She *hates* that name! We've known each other for a long time, Tessa. We went to school together up in Campbell Town, and to university together down here. The first day I met her, I called her Rachie and she told me if I ever called her that name again she'd punch me in the face. She was a bit more, well, unruly back then. But we all were. Comes from being in a small town, I think. The boredom was crushing. Well, I thought it was. Raphael liked the bush . . .'

Ms Hindmarsh trailed off, her face growing serious. 'Oh, listen to me, Tess,' she said, squeezing my arm. 'I've gone all nostalgic and sentimental! I promise you, I am a very competent and capable principal as well as being a complete sook!'

I returned her smile. I did like Ms Hindmarsh. Not as much as I like you, Connolly, but she seemed very nice, and I felt myself relaxing immediately. My breathing calmed down. My heartbeat slowed. I felt safe.

'Now, Tess, I think Rachel told you I've lined up a peer mentor for you to show you the ropes – how to get to your classes, where the bathrooms are, that sort of thing?'

I nodded. 'It's the daughter of one of Vinnie's friends?'

'Yes. She's the daughter of Edward Lord, one of the school's major benefactors. Her name is Charlotte. She is one of the prefects here at Cascade Falls. She is a really dedicated student, and very popular. I'm sure she will make an excellent guide for you. Ah, here she is!'

We finished our walk at the high, polished-wood entrance to the Cascade Falls building. Standing in front of it was a tall, slender girl with pale blonde hair pulled back in a neat, tight bun. Her face was very comely and I immediately felt inferior. She was how I imagined a lady would look; so refined and delicately pretty. Her cheekbones were very high and sharply angled, and every feature on her face seemed in exactly the right proportions – not too big or too small. It was only when I reached her eyes that I found a feature of her face that did not please me. They were the colour of a winter sky, and when her dark red lips smiled, her eyes did not follow, but stayed chilly. Perhaps that was how ladies smiled, though; always coldly in control. I smiled back awkwardly.

'Hello, Ms Hindmarsh,' she said.

She turned to me, and I felt my heart quicken, my muscles tense. She was smiling, but I did not feel she was being exactly friendly towards me.

And I was not sure if I felt friendly towards her.

I knew she was the daughter of Vinnie's friend. Of *your* friend. I knew Ms Hindmarsh had recommended her very highly, but still, something niggled at me. Something like a memory, but different. More like intuition.

'Hello . . . Tessa, is it?' she asked.

I nodded, and bowed my head. Every instinct in my body was telling me to make myself low.

Hide, a voice in my head said, and the muscles continued to pull down.

I pulled against them.

Camouflage. Stalk.

I told the voice in my head to be quiet. I tried to extinguish the fire that had begun to spark inside me.

Why was it asking me to hide? And especially, why was it asking me to hide from this girl?

Perhaps these voices were the call of memories trying to make themselves known – but now was not the time for them to be doing so. They were strange memories, belonging to a strange person, and I did not want to be seen as strange.

I had an inkling Charlotte Lord might not like 'strange'.

'Yes. Hello, Charlotte,' I said, willing my muscles to relax.

'Welcome to Cascade Falls,' she said, her eyes seeming to penetrate me. 'I know you'll get along just fine here. If you let me teach you how.'

'Did Miss Bloom give you a copy of Tessa's schedule?' asked Ms Hindmarsh.

Charlotte nodded and held up a sheet of blue paper. 'We have four classes together, so that's good,' she said. 'And I can ask one of the girls to keep an eye on her in the others. I think among all my friends there should be at least one girl in each of Tessa's classes. We'll look out for her. Dad told me everything Tessa has been through. He was most concerned for her.'

'You know everything that happened to me?' I blurted. 'Your father knows? But *how*?'

'Oh, my father knows most things,' Charlotte said, smiling in her pretty, wintry way.

Charlotte must have noticed my anxious expression, because she laughed and said, 'Don't worry, silly thing. Dad only told me you had an accident and they were unable to find your parents. If you have any more sordid skeletons in your closet, they are still hiding away behind the coats.'

I felt a bit calmer. Of course, she was right. There was no way her father could know everything – about my memory, about how I looked when I was discovered. About the scars.

For some reason, it was Charlotte knowing about the scars that bothered me most. I was not certain why, but I did not want her to know about the scars.

I did not want *any* of my classmates at Cascade Falls to know about the scars. I wanted to be normal. I wanted to be liked. I wanted to be successful at this 'school' business. I wanted to make you proud of me.

Suddenly, the wooden doors behind Charlotte sprang open and two giggling girls burst through.

One of the girls had quite dark skin, and another word joined the collection in my mind: *Aboriginal*.

She had very large eyes, shaped like round hazelnuts, and her cropped curly black hair was streaked with sunlight.

The other girl was very pale, with ginger hair and cheeks like two bright red apples. Her eyes were green and they were glimmering wickedly.

When the girls saw us standing there, they stopped abruptly and ceased their giggling.

'Sorry, Ms Hindmarsh,' said the short one. 'We were just, um, getting some fresh air before class!'

From deep inside the building, a voice echoed towards us.

'Laurel Simpson! Erin Mijak! Come back here!'

Ms Hindmarsh put her hands on her hips and stared at the girls, eyebrows raised.

'Ummm . . .' said the dark-skinned girl. 'Maybe we should just, errr . . .'

She looked behind her at the man with the messy, tawny hair and crumpled tweed suit who was rapidly approaching down the hallway, and then turned back to Ms Hindmarsh.

Another word popped into my head: *surrounded*.

The two girls seemed to deflate, their chests sinking, their faces becoming weary.

The short girl sighed and said, 'I'm sorry, Ms Hindmarsh. We got in trouble in the breakfast hall for making, um, *rude* things. Out of our pancakes.'

'We just wanted to see if we could do it!' the other girl blurted. 'I mean, we're getting really good with our mashed potato sculpture, and we just wanted to see if we could do it with pancakes, too, and it started *off* with just rabbits and angels and things, but then . . .

it was my fault. I wanted to see if I could make a pen–'

'Okay, enough, girls!' Ms Hindmarsh said, quickly. Her voice was a little bit harder than when she had been talking to me and Charlotte, but it still wasn't unkind. 'We have a new student here,' she said, putting a hand on my shoulder. It felt warm. 'We should be showing her what upstanding young women we have here at Cascade Falls. Do you think you're doing a very good job of that? Laurel?'

The red-haired girl shook her head, and her corkscrew auburn ringlets bounced and danced.

'Erin?'

The other girl said, 'No, Ms Hindmarsh. I'm sorry. It really was all my fault.'

'I don't really mind whose fault it is. It won't happen again, will it?'

'No, Ms Hindmarsh. I promise it won't,' said Lauren. 'Just, please, please, please don't give us another detention! We're already in detention until the middle of next month!'

I looked up at Ms Hindmarsh's face, and was surprised to see that she seemed to be trying not to smile. Her eyes were glittering, and the corners of her mouth were twitching up and down.

She looked behind the girls at the man in the tweed jacket, who was now standing in the doorway, hands on hips. He looked very, very cross. 'What do you think, Mr Beagle?' she asked.

'Well, *I* think the more time these two have in detention, thinking very hard about *actions* and *consequences,* the better! The way they behave is dreadful. And *dangerous.* They need to be more *vigilant.* Yes, more detention is just what they need.'

'I think they are already ashamed enough, don't you, Mr Beagle? To have acted in such a way in front of a new student?'

I looked at Laurel, and she gave me a small grin. One that looked anything but ashamed. I smiled shyly back.

'You're the boss,' said Mr Beagle grumpily. He turned to me and said, 'Welcome to Cascade Falls,' and then marched quickly back down the hallway.

Above me, seemingly from nowhere, a deafening noise blared out. The noise shocked me and I cowered, squeezing my eyes tightly shut. It sounded like some angry animal, threatening to pounce.

Ms Hindmarsh squeezed my shoulder. 'Sorry, Tessa, I'm afraid Miss Bloom hasn't *quite* got a handle on the new PA system yet. Her morning bells are always thunderous, or so quiet you can't hear them and so you turn up twenty minutes late. You can't use that as an excuse this time, though, Laurel and Erin. Come on, chop, chop!'

She raised an eyebrow at Laurel and Erin, who scampered quickly back up the stairs and into the hall.

From inside the hall, I could hear the thunder of many feet on a hard floor, and, before the door slammed shut again, I caught a glimpse of my new schoolmates.

So many of them! All shapes and sizes! And they were all dressed exactly as I was, in the charcoal grey uniform of Cascade Falls.

They all look so different from one another, I thought. *And yet the same. Perhaps I really can fit in here.*

'Well, Tessa, this is it,' said Ms Hindmarsh, squeezing my shoulder. 'Time to start your life as a student of Cascade Falls!'

CHapteR

SIX

WORDS I DID NOT KNOW BEFORE my fIRST DAY at Cascade Falls:

- netball (a team sport where balls are thrown from person to person and then into a hoop with a net on it)
- basketball (from what I can understand, exactly the same as netball, only you bang the ball against the ground sometimes and you can jump up when you throw the ball towards the net, which does seem a *bit* like cheating to me!)
- ball (for a little while, and then I remembered)
- bogan (it is a person of low morals and character – I think)

- Pepsi (a fizzy black drink that tastes a little bit like shoe polish)
- biro (a writing implement with ink *inside* it)
- LOL (this does not mean to lie about lazily. It means something is funny. It stands for 'laugh out loud'. I am not sure why people say it instead of actually laughing out loud)
- dude

The meaning of the last word I was still unsure of at the end of my first day at Cascade Falls. It was Laurel who said it to me, when she noticed me looking befuddled in our trigonometry class. She leaned over and whispered, 'It's okay, dude,' she said. 'Nobody gets this stuff.'

Later, as we left the classroom, I asked her what a 'dude' was. She just shrugged and said, 'It's, well, a dude. A dude's a dude. You know? Some things just are what they are. Like you. You're a Tessa. It would be pretty hard to explain what a *Tessa* is in one sentence, wouldn't it? You just are what you are and –'

She didn't get a chance to finish, before Charlotte Lord appeared at my side and said, 'It's okay, Laura.'

'Laurel.'

'Laurel. Sorry. I should remember that from the number of times I've seen your name on the detention list. Anyway, *Laurel*, you can go now. I'm Tessa's mentor. I can take it from here.'

'But . . . we were just talking, Charlotte,' Laurel protested.

Charlotte shook her head quickly and said, 'No thank you, Laurel. I have promised Ms Hindmarsh and my father that I will look after Tessa, and I believe a large component of this position will consist of preventing her forming acquaintances with undesirable persons . . .'

'Can you say that in English, please?' asked Laurel, which I thought was strange as it seemed that Charlotte was speaking very good English. At least I understood all the words she was saying – unlike 'dude' – even if they didn't seem to be very *nice* words.

Why did Charlotte dislike Laurel so much? She seemed nice – a bit naughty, but nice. And she was right. We *were* only talking.

'It means she reckons we're not good enough for her new toy,' said a voice from behind me.

I whirled around to see Laurel's friend, Erin, standing behind us.

'Come on, L,' she said flatly. 'Tessa probably just wants to hang out with her cool new friends, not us. Catch ya later, hey? If *Princess Charlotte* allows it.'

The two girls walked away.

I turned back to Charlotte to see her nostrils were flaring, ever so slightly, and her eyes were narrowed.

When she saw me looking, she opened her eyes up very wide and smiled.

'Don't mind those two,' she said. 'They're just bogans. Come on and I'll introduce you to some *nice* people.'

Beneath the huge oak tree in the middle of the school's central square (which *is* lovely, Connolly. You were right!), I met Kelly, Amy, Jenna, Bridget, Claudia and Inga.

'This is our outside place,' Charlotte said. 'Inside, we have our own table in the cafeteria.'

'Does everyone?' I asked.

Charlotte laughed. 'Of course not,' she said. She waved at the group as we approached and raised her voice slightly. 'Girls, this is Tessa.'

None of them smiled with their eyes, and yet they spoke as though they were glad to meet me.

'So, so, *so* wonderful to meet you, Tessa!' squealed Kelly, bobbing up and down like a strange, overexcited puppy.

'I hope you're enjoying it here,' said Amy, her eyes narrowed and her arms crossed over her chest. 'You've certainly fallen on your feet getting Charlotte as a mentor.'

'Very lucky,' said Bridget.

'Lovely to have a new girl,' said Claudia, smiling in a way that seemed warmer than when Charlotte smiled. I decided I liked Claudia the best. She looked somewhat like a very pretty, raven-haired elf.

Inga I liked less. Her eyes were like sapphires and every bit as hard, and her hair was short and severe and nearly as pale as Charlotte's. When Charlotte introduced us, she didn't smile or greet me; she just stood staring, one eyebrow raised as if to say, 'Do you really think you belong here?'

I felt like telling her that no, I didn't. Not really.

The girls were very pretty, but talking to them for only a few minutes made me feel very tired and inadequate. They all spoke with such plummy accents, as though they had been raised in a manor in England, not a convict town at the end of the world. Charlotte explained that they had all been sent to finishing classes, courtesy of her father. 'Which is why we stand a mile above the other girls at Cascade Falls,' she said. 'This may be an exclusive school, but many of its population would make you believe otherwise.' She leaned in and whispered, 'Scholarship students,' and made a repulsed face. 'They bring down the tone of exclusivity quite severely!'

Exclusive. That word seemed perfect for Charlotte and her friends. They were exclusive. They were important.

And they seemed to be keenly aware of it. I wanted to like them. I promised myself I would *try* to like them. But as we walked away from the oak tree and the thoroughbred girls, I found myself feeling slightly, secretly, relieved.

Then Charlotte introduced me to Rhiannah.

Rhiannah's hair was jet black, and her skin was as white as the sheets on my hospital bed. Her eyes were dark, too. Nearly black. And when Charlotte introduced us, Rhiannah's dark pink lips curled upwards and her eyes smiled too.

'This is Tessa,' Charlotte said, for perhaps the twentieth time. It felt like the millionth and I was growing tired of the sound of my own name. 'She's new. Tessa, this is Rhiannah.'

Rhiannah wrinkled up her nose and sniffed at the air.

'Is there a problem, Rhiannah?' asked Charlotte testily.

'No, no, not at all,' said Rhiannah. 'I just thought I smelled . . . something. Don't mind me.'

Rhiannah held out her hand and took mine. She shook it up and down. Her grip was strong, but I matched it. 'Lovely hands,' she said, still smiling.

I looked down at them. To my eyes, the fingers look stubby and the fingernails were too short and remained dirty, no matter how many times you and I scrubbed at them. Remember, Connolly? You said they looked like farmers' fingernails.

'Why are they lovely?' I asked.

Rhiannah just shrugged and smiled again. 'They look like they're used for great things. You can tell a lot about a person from their hands.'

I examined my hands more closely. They had wide, square palms, and the fingernails looked tough – as if they could claw through anything. Rhiannah's were a bit like that, too: long and slightly pointed and dark. I looked at Charlotte's fingernails. They were pearly pink and they sparkled in the sun.

I liked mine better.

'That's a very charming bangle,' I said, looking at the metal circle around her wrist. I said it partly because I felt as though I should compliment her back after she had been so nice to me, and partly because I really did like it.

The bangle was made from flat, shiny copper. It looked like she polished it every day. Carved into its surface were intricate patterns that looked somehow like . . . animal tracks?

A word tried to push its way into the group of words inside my mind.

It started with a 'P'.

Poor . . . Purr . . .

Purinin . . .

I could not draw my eyes away from the bangle. It seemed, strangely, as though as I was looking at it, the patterns began to move – the footprints began to leap and dance. Almost as though my brain were not in control of my limbs, I reached out. I wanted to touch it. I just wanted to find out what it would *feel* like. It was as if I was under some strange sort of spell.

Rihannah jerked her hand away, breaking the enchantment. 'Don't touch that . . . please,' she said. I looked up at her eyes. They seemed fearful. I wondered why. All I had wanted was to touch the bangle. I looked back down at it again now. The footprints were standing still. The magic was over.

'Tessa?'

'Yes?' I said, looking up at Charlotte.

'Time to move on,' she said. 'See you later, Rhiannah.'

'Yeah, I gotta go too. My brother's waiting for me,' said Rhiannah. Her voice was back to normal now. 'Great to meet you, Tessa!'

I watched Rhiannah walk towards the school gates. As they opened, I saw a boy standing on the other side. His hair was dark, like Rhiannah's. Even from here I could see that he was exceedingly handsome. As the gates shut, I was almost certain I saw his eyes flick my way, and his brow furrow. I felt my heart begin to beat very quickly, and I pressed my hand to my chest, feeling my cheeks burn.

'He's a bit of a looker, isn't he?' Charlotte whispered in my ear. 'I don't blame you for checking him out.'

'I was doing nothing of the sort!' I protested.

'Oh, come on. Perrin is famous,' said Charlotte. 'One of the best-looking boys in Hobart. Pity his sister is such a nutcase. I hope she didn't scare you. I only introduced you so you didn't get freaked out by her later.'

I shook Perrin's face from my head. I wanted to tell Charlotte that I didn't think Rhiannah seemed weird at all. She seemed much nicer than all the ones who didn't smile with their eyes.

But before I could say anything, the loud noise that had scared me so much that morning quaked through the air yet again. It scared me less each time. I flinched, but I did not cower.

Charlotte clapped her hands. 'Class time!' she said. 'I do hope you have enjoyed meeting my friends, Tessa. They are definitely the most *correct* people for you to be associating with at Cascade Falls. I hope you will understand now that Erin and Laurel, and Rhiannah and her crowd are, well, *not*. You'll thank me later for teaching you this, trust me. Now, according to your schedule, you have maths, with me. Come on. We mustn't be late.'

I trailed along behind Charlotte as she marched up the long, polished wood floorboards of the corridor towards our classroom, watching as the sun through the windows glinted off her spun-gold hair. I couldn't help thinking that the halo of light did look very much like a crown.

'*Princess Charlotte,*' Erin had called her.

I wondered then whether the Tessa who came out of the bush, with her matted hair and bruises and the long streaking scars across her back, would have seemed like the kind of girl Princess Charlotte would want in her court.

I wondered if the Tessa from *now* would be, if Charlotte could see who she really was.

After all, I still had the scars.

CHAPTER

seven

AS I LAY IN MY NEW BED ON THE FIRST NIGHT IN MY NEW school, the scars came alive.

It was late – around midnight, but my body felt as though it was midday. My mind was alert and my eyes didn't want to close. There was too much to think about.

What a big, strange day it had been!

The rest of my classes had been agreeable. Some were even informative and interesting. I had kept quiet and attentive and I believed I had made a good impression on my teachers. I even answered a question or two! School, it seemed, was not so odd and difficult after all. At lunch time, Charlotte and her friends had some sort of rehearsal, so I sat by myself in the sun and watched my schoolmates congregate and cluster and move about like a flock of grey pigeons. I enjoyed watching them, knowing I was one of them too. I liked feeling as though I was part of something. Like I belonged.

The evening had gone quite well also. I sat with Charlotte and her friends at dinner and even made some conversation. I complimented the food (and kept my mouth closed when the others ranted about how 'greasy' and fattening it was). I remarked that it was a pretty night outside (and stared at my plate as the others complained about the cold). Though they disagreed with my opinions, the other girls didn't seem angry at me. In fact, Claudia even squeezed my hand at one point and said, 'You're doing well, Tessa.'

That made me feel happy. *Accepted.*

When the conversation turned to fashions and 'celebrities', the voices of the girls muted somewhat. I did not understand why 'leggings as trousers – cool or not?' was an interesting topic, and I was also ignorant as to why the other girls seemed interested in talking about the romances and scandals of people they didn't even know. I checked that I would not be missed from the conversation and, once I had concluded that they were too enthralled in a discussion on the physique of a renowned male musician (they called him a 'pop star'), I retreated inside my head.

And in there was Cat. I wondered if she had sat at this same table, having similar conversations. I wondered how many of the girls here knew her. I wondered if I should ask them, or if they might be sensitive about her disappearance. I imagined her, cold and alone, in the wilderness.

I *never* imagined her dead, though I knew it was logically possible. Perhaps it was only hope for you, Connolly. Perhaps I just *wanted* Cat to be alive but . . . I don't know how to describe it. It was almost intuition. I sensed that she was out there. Odd and mad and *witching* as it may seem, I somehow *knew*. And I also knew it was up to me to find her. It was like the dreams I had been having since I awoke – the ones that seemed so real and yet so implausible; it was as though my subconscious knew things my consciousness did not. I could not explain it, but I could not argue with it either. The feeling was so strong. Cat *was alive*.

'Tessa?' A sharp voice punctured my contemplation. My eyes snapped towards Inga, whose own eyes were boring into me. 'I asked you a question,' she said.

'I'm sorry,' I said. 'I think I am quite tired. What was your question?'

Inga rolled her eyes. 'I just wanted to know if you have a boyfriend?'

'A boyfriend?' I asked. The term was unfamiliar to me. Was Inga asking if I had any male companions? Was she implying I had been improper?

'Yes, you know,' she said slowly, as though I was dimwitted. 'A boyfriend?'

'You don't have to answer that, Tessa,' said Claudia, gently. She turned to Inga. 'That's private,' she said.

'Aww, but I thought we were friends,' Inga said, her voice dripping with sarcasm. I really did not like Inga. 'All right,' she said. 'I'll share first. I have a boyfriend. His name is Jakob. He's completely hot and he kisses like a demon.'

Ah, so Inga was not simply talking about male companions. She was talking about . . . gentlemen callers. About suitors.

'I . . . I don't really know if I have a boyfriend,' I replied, truthfully. I had not remembered a boyfriend. I could not remember *any* boys. But, like my *feeling* about Cat, I had a sense that perhaps there had been someone. Dancing around my brain was a hint of a musky smell; the feeling of lips brushing against mine. Maybe this *was* just a dream, though. After all, I had seen myself in the mirror after I was rescued. What boy would have wanted me?

'Right,' said Inga, her eyes narrowing. 'Weird.'

I felt my cheeks colour. It *was* weird to not know if you had a suitor. I chastised myself and vowed to be more mindful in my future conversations.

'It's not weird,' said Claudia, soothingly. 'There have been heaps of times in my life when I haven't really known if a boy was my boyfriend. They can be pigs sometimes, can't they, Tessa?'

I nodded, yawning as I did so and Amy snapped, 'Sorry for keeping you up, Tessa.' She flicked her streaky blonde hair over her shoulder and looked at Inga, who rolled her eyes.

'She's had a big day,' Claudia said, touching me gently on the arm.

It was true. I'd had a big day. I was tired. But, later, when I was lying on my side on my new bed, in my new room, in my new school, sleep seemed a million miles away.

My new roommate was not in her bed. She was away on a bushwalking trip. Ms Hindmarsh had told me this when she showed me to my room, earlier in the evening, but still, I was disappointed. I wanted to meet her.

Ms Hindmarsh told me that her name was Rhiannah. This cheered me. I assumed (and secretly hoped), that there was only one Rhiannah, the one Charlotte had introduced me to, the one with the black hair and the pretty bangle. I remembered Charlotte calling her strange, but Rhiannah seemed nice to me. I thought she would make a pleasant roommate.

'Rhiannah is a bit of a nature nut,' Ms Hindmarsh had explained. 'Loves the bush.'

'Me too,' I said, again without thinking, and the next words to come into my mind were, *How do you know that, Tessa?*

Ms Hindmarsh didn't ask how I knew that, though. She just squeezed my shoulder and said, 'Great! Well, you'll have lots to talk about, won't you? I really hope you get along. I would, ideally, have liked you to bunk down with one of the prefects, but they all have roommates already, and I wouldn't like to cause disruptions to their lives and routines. They're all very conscientious students, and I'm aware that disruption can be detrimental to academic progress.'

'Rhiannah didn't mind being disrupted?' I asked. 'She didn't mind her other roommate moving out?'

'Her other roommate had . . . already gone,' said Ms Hindmarsh, and a curious darkness settled on her face. I remembered what you said, Connolly, about Ms Hindmarsh's husband being 'gone'. You hadn't said 'dead'. Just 'gone'. There seemed to be so much uncertainty in that word – so much emptiness, as though the word was made of air. Rhiannah's roommate was 'gone'. Ms Hindmarsh's husband was 'gone'. My parents were 'gone'. Cat was 'gone'. They were like leaves, blown quietly away by a summer breeze. I didn't know what to say to Ms Hindmarsh. I wanted to tell her I would help to find her husband too, but I knew my first priority was to find Cat. Maybe one would lead to the other.

As quickly as the darkness appeared, brightness came again and Ms Hindmarsh smiled. 'Anyway, Tessa, make yourself at home,' she said, as she opened the door to room 36. 'I know you don't have many things with you but I'm sure you'll settle in soon and find some way to make it yours.'

I looked around the room. 'Does Rhiannah not have many "things" either?' I asked.

The room looked very comfortable, but its furniture and decorations were decidedly minimal. The furniture consisted of two beds with thick charcoal-coloured quilts and dark pillows, two armchairs, a black box which I took to be some sort of electronic equipment (the operation of which I would have to sneakily ascertain at a later time), a deep-red rug on the floor, two small wooden bedside tables, two charcoal reading lamps, a wood-framed mirror on the wall, two tall wooden wardrobes and a strange, misshapen black splodge in the corner.

'A beanbag,' Ms Hindmarsh said, as if reading my mind. 'For your guests to sit on. I'm afraid we couldn't quite spring for three armchairs per room, and a beanbag is more comfortable than a plastic chair, I suppose. I don't know; it was the interior decorator's idea.'

A 'beanbag'?

The word squeezed into my mind with the other words, but it looked uncomfortable there. As if it wasn't sure of its place or purpose. As if it *knew* it looked a bit funny and silly.

I wondered whose idea it was that chairs were a less than ideal apparatus for sitting on, and that a wonky, bean-filled splodge might be a more sensible idea. The thought made me smile. I wondered if the gentleman who had created it was now very rich and famous, like the man who invented the refrigerator, or mechanical sheep clippers!

My eyes moved away from the funny beanbag to other features of the room. There was one picture on the wall – a painting of a Tasmanian devil. The image looked as though the creature might be slightly fearsome, but I didn't feel scared by it. In fact, I thought it was strangely beautiful.

'Yes, she does love her devils,' said Ms Hindmarsh when she saw me looking at the picture. 'But she calls them *purinina*, which is the Aboriginal name for them.'

Purinina.

That was the word that had been trying to squeeze into my head before, when I was talking to Rhiannah.

Strange that the word I had been trying to think of would turn out to be the name of Rhiannah's favourite thing.

'She's always drawing them in art class,' Ms Hindmarsh went on. 'And she helps out at the market, selling scarves and badges and things to raise money for them. It's very important to her. Maybe you can talk to her about it? I'm sure she'd love to tell you. I hope you'll be happy here with her, Tessa.'

Later, staring through the darkness at Rhiannah's empty bed, I hoped so too.

And niggling in the back of my mind was another hope.

If Rhiannah liked bushwalking, maybe she knew Cat. Maybe she was there on the bushwalk when Cat went missing. Maybe she knew something about what happened.

I wondered if she might tell me what she knew, and if it might be the first clue to finding Cat.

I also wondered about the pair of shiny brown hiking boots sitting neatly side by side beside Rhiannah's bed. If Rhiannah was on a bushwalk, why hadn't she taken her boots with her? I pictured her, running through the trees, barefoot and wild. My stomach pulsed with yearning.

CHAPTER
EIGHT

IT WAS TOO HOT IN THE ROOM. IT WAS LIKE THE HOSPITAL — heated far too well, though nobody else ever seemed to notice. I was sweating.

I looked over at the window on Rhiannah's side of the room. The crack in the dark-red curtain gifted me a beguiling glimpse of the cool night sky. I felt the hairs on my back stand up; my pulse quicken. I wanted to jump out. I wanted to run through the playground, through the sporting fields, through the high metal gates and away, into the bush that surrounded Cascade Falls, into the trees and moss and bracken and dirt and rocks and wild water.

I padded across the room and perched on the corner of Rhiannah's armchair. I pressed my hand against the window. It was cool to my touch.

I opened it just a little bit, and then turned the latch backwards to lock it. I didn't want my instincts to take over my logic; to allow my body to follow my longing to push the window wide open and leap. I knew my instincts to be powerful. In the days since I had been rescued I had, many times, felt compelled to do things my brain told me were illogical or even dangerous. I remembered biting the nurse. I remembered the fire that sometimes smouldered in my belly, crackling and simmering, making me want to run away from the hospital and into the wilderness. I knew I was capable of madness. I didn't want it to compel me out of the window.

Despite my initial misgivings, I liked my room, my school, my new life.

I didn't want to leave.

But the night air was intoxicating.

I breathed it in and it seemed to fill not only my nostrils but my entire body, from my scalp right down to my toes. It smelled of wet grass and bark and dirt and something else. Something without words. Something *wild*.

I wanted to roll in the dirt. I wanted to hurtle through the trees. I wanted to *sniff things*.

I wondered if the other girls felt these urges, or if they were unique to me. I could not imagine Charlotte Lord wishing to leap out of a window. I wondered if the old me – the one before my accident – would have just leapt without thinking.

My body pulsed and shuddered and I willed it to still. Something told me I needed to control myself if I was to fit in here at Cascade Falls.

And if I was to find Cat.

A voice whispered inside my mind. *Howl*, it hissed. *Bay. Growl.*

'No,' I whispered out loud. 'I am in control.'

The words felt familiar, like a mantra or a hymn. I was certain I had said them before. But what had I needed to control? This same burning, fevered desire to break out? What had I been trapped in before? What was I trapped in *now*?

I stretched out my fingers against the glass and allowed my eyes to blur. It seemed like my hand was part of the sky. Then, as I watched, half-squinting, my fingernails seemed to lengthen, my fingers curled up . . .

Like paws. I gasped, blinking quickly, and looked closely at my fingers. They were normal. An eerie, unsettled feeling remained.

I looked up at the sky, letting it soothe me. It was beautiful. I couldn't see much of it above the high stone walls, but it was enough. The stars were like glimmering specks of sand, and the moon was almost full. It looked like an apple that had been peeled on only one side.

'Hello, moon,' I whispered, and my words flew out on the night air and up into the sky.

CHAPTER

NINE

I DIDN'T SLEEP VERY MUCH THAT FIRST NIGHT, BUT WHEN
I did, I dreamed again one of my odd, unsettling dreams.

I was floating in the sky overlooking a large building in
the middle of a wide, green valley guarded by craggy hills.

As I slowly drifted down towards it, I saw that nestled
in the valley was a thin snake of buildings coiling around
flat, muddy courtyards. The courtyards reminded me of
the yard out the front of Cascade Falls, where you had
stopped your car, and the trees seemed familiar too. The
buildings I knew also, but it was a hazy memory. I felt
strangely as though I had seen them on our car journey
and yet I knew they did not look like any of the buildings
you pointed out to me.

They did not look like they were part of your world.

As I flew farther down, I saw a young girl sitting hunched against the wall of one of the buildings. She was dressed very differently from the girls here at Cascade Falls – in a long pale cotton dress and a cloth cap.

Her head was bowed and her face was hidden by her long hair.

Her hands were grasping at the cloth of her dress, wringing it and then smoothing it out, over and over again.

She sniffed loudly and looked up, her face angled away from me and still obscured by hair. I could see only part of a cheek, slick with tears.

'Stop it!' she whispered. 'Stop crying! You don't cry!'

She rubbed at her face, roughly, then shook her head so suddenly that my dream self was startled. 'It's not true,' she said. 'It's not true. They're lying to me again. It can't be true. It's not true.'

She looked up and off to the left, and I could feel that another presence was there. I tried to turn and see who it was, but my eyes were fixed on the girl.

'Is it true? What they say? That she's gone?' she asked, her voice gritty. Then she shook her head again, her hair hanging in front of her face like a mourning veil.

'No!' she growled. 'No, it's not. It's not . . .'

Sobs took her body captive, and she tried to rock herself free.

When she spoke again, all traces of her girlish voice had gone, and the sound was like a howl. 'Please,' she begged the invisible one. 'I'm all alone now. I have seen what you have done! I know what you can do! Do it to me. I will join you. I will help you! Please! If you don't take me with you . . . if I am here alone, I will die. I am strong. I will prove it. I know you think I am weak, but that is only what she wanted you to think. She wanted to protect me, can't you see? I would have joined you long ago! Please don't leave me here like this!'

The girl pushed herself to her feet and I could feel the pain searing her palms as the jagged gravel bit and scratched them. She didn't seem to notice.

She walked quickly towards me, towards the invisible one, and as she did so, the edges of my vision began to blur. Shadows crept in and I began to drift away.

I was floating above her, far away, when I heard her final cry.

'Please!'

I was up in the sky now. The moon was full and plump and the stars gave me just enough light to see the girl. Another shape moved towards her; fast and taut and terrifying. It was a monster. Even from so far away, I could see that it was a monster, and I opened my mouth and let out a silent scream.

The girl didn't scream, though. She just stood there and watched as the monster leapt at her, and made her disappear.

I shook and shuddered, and the sky around me bubbled and quaked and then, all of a sudden, there was light, blinding and piercing and horrible, and I couldn't see anything any more.

And the air was full of my screaming.

cHapteR
teN

WHEN I OPENED my eyes, a paLe face fiLLeD my vision.

Of course, I screamed blue murder! And, of course, the other girl screamed too. It would have seemed very comical from the outside. From the inside, it was wholly terrifying!

Then, the other girl stopped screaming and started laughing hysterically.

And then I recognised her face. 'Rhiannah?' I said.

She nodded. She was still laughing so hard that tears were streaming down her face. 'I'm so sorry, love. It's just –' She broke off as giggles took over again. Despite myself, I could feel the corners of my mouth begin to push upwards.

'What?' I said.

Rhiannah took a deep breath and opened her dark eyes wide. 'Right, Rin. Focus. Tessa, I'm sorry for scaring the crap out of you. I didn't mean to. You were just making funny noises and I was worried. Sorry.'

Her lips twitched but she controlled them.

'It's okay,' I said. 'I think I was just having a bad dream.'

Rhiannah offered a hand to help me up. 'Whoa. That's some grip you've got there,' she said, shaking her hand. 'I noticed it yesterday. Did you do bodybuilding at your old school?'

I looked down at my hand, flexing it. I tried to ignore the memory of last night's hallucination; the one where my hands had become paws. My hands were normal. I had thought Rhiannah's grip strong as well. If *my* strength was abnormal, then hers was equally so.

'Hey, it's okay. I'm just teasing,' said Rhiannah, smiling. 'I'm pretty fit myself. It's not a bad thing. You wanna tell me what your nightmare was about?'

I shook my head. Part of me wanted to tell her about the monster and the screaming but another part of me worried she might not understand. She was an ordinary girl. I was sure she did not dream of beasts and howling. My face flushed as I lied, 'I'm not really sure.'

Rhiannah grinned. 'Yeah, I have dreams like that all the time. Isn't it frustrating when you wake up and you can't remember a single thing? You okay now, roomie?'

'I'm okay now, roomie,' I replied. I liked the way the word felt in my mouth. It felt friendly. I couldn't imagine Charlotte Lord saying 'roomie'.

Rhiannah grabbed a bunch of her thick, dark hair and shoved it roughly behind her ear. I noticed that she had a small scratch on her forehead just below her hairline and a streak of mud above her nose.

'Did you hurt yourself on your bushwalk?' I asked.

'What?' Rhiannah's hand rushed to her forehead. 'Oh. Yeah, I guess so. Those bushwalks can get pretty rowdy!'

And right then I wanted to ask, 'How rowdy can they get? Was it rowdy on the day Connolly's daughter disappeared?'

But maybe it was too soon.

Maybe I should wait for a little while before I asked. Rhiannah seemed very nice, but I should get to know her a little bit better before I decided whether I could trust her.

Rhiannah grinned. Then she put a hand on my shoulder and said, 'Listen, mate, I'm sorry I wasn't here to, you know, welcome you to Casa Rhiannah and all.'

'Casa Rhiannah?'

She rolled her eyes. 'It's what my mates Harriet and Sara started calling it, because I lived here alone. Like a weird, crazy old loser hermit! I guess now we can call it Casa Rhiannah Tessa. Has a nice ring to it, don't you think?'

'Yes,' I replied, shyly.

'So anyway,' Rhiannah went on, smiling, 'It's getting pretty close to breakfast time, so we should think about heading. I'm totally stuffed. I didn't get in 'til two, and you were dead to the world with no blankets on. You don't like blankets?'

'I was too hot.'

'Yeah, they overheat the crap out of these rooms. I have no idea why. Maybe Princess Charlotte complained about it being too cold once.'

'You call her that, too?' I asked. 'Erin called her that.'

'*Everybody* calls her that. Charlotte Lord is the biggest princess this side of England. I feel so sorry for you, having to have her as your mentor.'

'She's not so bad,' I said, feeling like I should defend Charlotte. After all, she had been very helpful to me yesterday, showing me where everything was, and where to go, and how to act, and introducing me to people I should know.

'She's not so bad because you haven't got on her bad *side* yet. And, trust me, that's really easy to do. Charlotte has very . . . particular ideas about what she likes and doesn't like. It's very easy to piss her off.'

'Piss her off?'

I hadn't heard that expression before. I mean, I had heard the word 'piss' used as another word for urination, but I assumed (and hoped) that Rhiannah *wasn't* talking about urination. That would be rather odd. And unsanitary.

'You know, make her angry,' said Rhiannah.

'Strange expression,' I murmured.

'Yeah, I suppose it is.' She nodded thoughtfully. 'Anyway, enough about Her Royal Up-herself-ness. Just take the warning on board, okay? If you want to be all matey mate with her, that's your choice and I won't think any less of you, but just, you know, be careful. And I would also advise against telling her anything personal. That girl might only be a princess in most ways, but she is definitely the *queen* of gossip at Cascade Falls. Be a bit wary, okay?'

'I will,' I said, nodding.

'Right! Now we've sorted that one out, what is your stance on waffles?'

'Waffles?'

Another word I didn't know. I wondered if it had something to do with urination too. I hoped not.

'Oh, geez! Wow. You don't know waffles? Seriously? Okay, mate. Here's the plan: we get up, we go and shower –'

'Shower?'

I could feel the scars on my back begin to burn and throb. I winced. They'd hurt before, but not like this. The pain was bad, but my anxiety was worse.

I didn't want to shower.

I didn't want anybody else to see my scars.

I didn't want them to think I was *strange*.

My heart started beating very quickly and the palms of my hands felt sticky with sweat. 'Do we . . . I mean . . . the showers . . .'

'Oh, they're really good showers here, don't worry!' said Rhiannah. 'If you've been to other boarding schools, with cold water, or water that cuts out after a minute or, you know, no shower curtains or whatever, this is not like that. You get your very own big stall, and those posh nozzles where you can change the water pressure, and they have swanky smelly shampoo and soap and moisturiser in these pump things that stick on the wall, and heated towel racks and everything! It's heaven!'

'So, it's private?' I asked. I didn't care about water pressure or pump things or hot towels. All I wanted to know was that nobody else was going to see my scars.

'Oh, yeah!' said Rhiannah, smiling. 'No ripping back the curtains to check you're washing properly here. I mean, you have a timer so you don't waste water, but that's about it. So, plan? Shower time and then waffle time?'

'I really do want to know what a waffle *is* before I say it is waffle time,' I said, firmly. I didn't want to get myself into anything unsavoury.

Rhiannah rolled her eyes. 'Can't you just trust me? No? Okay, it's a breakfast item. And it's good. That's all I'm going to tell you. Is that enough?'

I nodded. 'That's enough.'

'Well, thank Mother Earth for that. Shall we go?'

Rhiannah held out a pale hand to me and I took it. I watched as the copper bangle slid down her arm and settled on her wrist. Her eyes followed me. 'It's a family thing,' she said, very casually considering the way she had reacted yesterday. 'An heirloom. You really like it, don't you?'

I nodded.

'That's a worry,' she said.

CHAPTER

eLeveN

HAVE YOU EVER HAD WAFFLES, CONNOLLY?

If you haven't, and I mean this with the utmost fervour and seriousness, you really *must do it!*

Waffles are just the most wondrous thing that was ever invented! They are crunchy and yet soft; sweet and yet savoury; filling and yet oh, so very light and I loved them so much I had four! With ice cream as well! The smell of them hit me long before I reached the dining hall (the *cafeteria*). 'Oh, they smell wonderful!' I exclaimed.

'You can smell them already?' asked Rhiannah, her eyebrows raised, and I was reminded yet again how things – sights, smells, noises – happen more powerfully for me than for others. I was embarrassed again, but the feeling faded as soon as I took my first bite. I swear to you,

Connolly, I had never eaten anything so heavenly. If it wasn't for the fear that I might get fat, and *weak,* I would have eaten *five* waffles!

As I ate, I looked about the cafeteria at my new schoolmates. I was disconcerted to see that some of them were looking back at me. Some smiled when I caught their eye. Some looked away quickly and whispered to their friends.

'They're just interested in you 'cos you're new,' said Rhiannah's friend Harriet. 'It was the same when *we* started. Don't worry about it. They'll get sick of you.'

I nodded mutely. I could feel my heart quickening, and a prickle of sweat on the back of my neck. The cafeteria was just a bit too busy. There were too many people. I was used to quiet.

The hospital was quiet.

And maybe I had liked quiet *before* as well. My aversion to the bustle and clatter seemed to come from deep within me.

I am Tessa. I like quiet.

'Of course, you know they're completely bad for you,' said Rhiannah, pointing at the waffle suspended midway to my mouth. 'You'll be as round as a wombat if you eat even one more. And then Princess Charlotte will definitely hate you. Although, to be honest, I actually don't think she likes you all that much right now. Not that that's a bad thing.'

'Why doesn't she like me?' I asked, swinging my head around to look for Charlotte's table.

Sure enough, Charlotte and every single one of her pretty friends were very obviously glowering at me. It was quite a terrifying sight.

'What did I do wrong?' I asked, looking back at Rhiannah and her friends.

'You sat with us instead of her,' said Harriet, shrugging and looking at me as though I were stupid for not realising this myself.

Harriet was one of Rhiannah's two best friends. She had dark hair, like Rhiannah's, but hers had sunny streaks running through the black. Her eyes were lighter than Rhiannah's – a sort of golden brown. Her features were all quite sharp, but her face was friendly. She was taller than Rhiannah, and very thin and wiry. She looked like she should be a long distance runner. 'Field sports, actually,' she'd said, smiling, when I asked. 'Long jump, javelin, triple jump. You name it. I'm not really all that into shot put. I don't have the leg strength for it. But, apart from that, if it's a field sport, it's my bag.'

'Your bag?' I asked, wondering how a sport could also be a bag.

'My *thing*, you know? I love it!' She grinned so hard I thought her face would break in two, and I liked her immediately, nearly as much as Rhiannah.

Rhiannah's other best friend was called Sara. Sara wore thick-framed glasses and wore her black ringlets in pigtail bunches on the sides of her head. Her face was rounder than Harriet's, and softer, and it wore a permanently perplexed and anxious expression. When she talked, it was at a pace so rapid I sometimes had trouble making out one word from another.

I immediately noticed that both of the girls were wearing copper bangles like Rhiannah's, but with slightly different patterns on them. I loved those bangles. I wanted one very badly. I wondered if perhaps, should I become very good friends with Rhiannah and the others, they might let me have one too.

But Rhiannah had said that her bangle was a family heirloom.

Perhaps Rhiannah and Harriet and Sara were related. Perhaps they were cousins, and the bangles were some sort of family tradition. The girls did all look quite similar, with their pale skin and dark hair and eyes. I asked Rhiannah.

'Nope,' she said. 'It's just that all the best people have black hair.'

My hand shot up to my own sandy crop, and Rhiannah laughed and said, 'Well, apart from you, obviously! Though, you know, a couple of shades lighter and you'd be in Princess Charlotte territory, and we really don't wanna go there.'

I could feel Princess Charlotte's eyes stabbing two large holes in the back of my head, like icicle daggers.

'Is that really it?' I asked. 'Is she glaring because I am sitting with you? Because she didn't seem to mind at all when I asked her.'

Charlotte had just cocked her pretty head to one side and said, 'Really? Rhiannah? You'd prefer to sit with her?'

'She's my roommate,' I replied. 'And she promised to teach me about waffles. If you would prefer me to sit with you . . .'

'No, no! Of course! You sit with Rhiannah, if that's what you *really* want,' Charlotte said, smiling, as usual, with her mouth and not her eyes.

'Thanks!' I said, and dashed off to Rhiannah and my waffles.

At the time, it seemed like everything was fine. As I thought back, though, I could hear a tiny hint of scorn in Charlotte's voice; a tenseness to her smile.

'She's not going to act hurt in front of her friends, is she?' said Rhiannah. 'That wouldn't be cool. That would make her look like she cared about you which, obviously, if you are going to hang out with us, she won't any more.'

'Why would that be so?' I asked, feeling quite bewildered.

'Because Charlotte knows what she likes, and she doesn't like us. She likes pink, and she likes Sarah

Brightman and Vanessa Mae, and she likes maths and science, but she's not very keen on any of the arty subjects, and she likes her hair in a bun, or in a braid, and she likes tinned peaches but not waffles, and she thinks reading anything other than books for school is a waste of time, and she is allowed to have a television in her room because the people in her common room were getting sick of her only wanting to watch English period dramas, and she doesn't like us because we're not perfect, and so if you hang around with us *you* won't be perfect either, and also, you would have betrayed her by choosing to be with us instead of her and her friends, and so she will probably hate you,' said Sara.

She said it without taking one single breath, and I felt as if my brain was going to explode from absorbing so many words in so little time.

'Was your old school really small?' asked Harriet. 'I mean, this stuff is "clique 101": "Don't mess with the in-crowd or they will mess you back". It's the first thing you learn in high school. I'm guessing your old school was small, so you didn't have cliques?'

'Yes,' I said, not trusting myself to elaborate more.

'Right,' said Sara, smiling. 'I was wondering why you were so clueless.'

I turned around and looked at Charlotte again.

She was still staring at me and I felt cold all over.

Part of me wanted to walk straight over to her and say, 'I'm sorry, Charlotte. I shouldn't have sat with Harriet and Sara and Rhiannah. I will definitely sit with you from now on. Just please, stop glaring at me like that. It's scary.'

A bigger part, though, thought of how Charlotte and her friends didn't smile with their eyes, and how they only talked about boys and makeup and clothes, and how it bored me, and how sitting with Harriet and Sara and Rhiannah and eating waffles was much more fun.

If I *had* sat with Charlotte, I might not have been allowed to eat waffles. And that would have been a tragedy.

I also didn't really think I *wanted* to be friends with someone who wouldn't let me be friends with anyone except the people she *told* me I could be friends with.

And I definitely didn't want to be friends with someone who wanted perfection. I thought of my scars, and the way my instincts sometimes told me to do strange things – to bay and howl. I thought of my lost memories. I thought of the memories I *did* have, about being discovered on a mountain looking like a cave-person. If Charlotte knew all that, I was certain she would not think me perfect.

I looked away from Charlotte's table back towards Rhiannah and her friends, and I smiled at them. 'I don't mind,' I said. 'I don't mind if she hates me. As long as I have waffles everything will be okay.'

Rhiannah snorted. 'You're hilarious!' she said. She put a pale hand on my forearm. 'Seriously, though, mate, you'll have us as well, okay? You're my roommate. I've got your back.'

'My back?' I blurted, feeling my heart quicken and my muscles tense.

'Yeah, you know. We'll look out for you,' said Harriet.

My body melted with relief.

'Thanks,' I said.

Rhiannah put squeezed my arm. 'We'll protect you from the evil princess,' she said. 'We can be pretty tough, when we want to be.'

cHapter
twelve

I DIDN'T take RHIANNAH AND HER fRIENDS WHOLLy
seriously when they said I might need protecting from
Charlotte. She was, after all, only a girl, and I hadn't done
anything *really* bad to offend her or make her dislike me.

At least, I didn't think I had. I wasn't rude or impolite.
I was very courteous and grateful for all of her help.

And yet she seemed very quickly to go from friend to
enemy. It was horrible, Connolly! One moment, she was
hooking her arm through mine and showing me to her
friends as though I was some sort of prize, and the next
she had turned against me like a contrary wind.

I first got an inkling of it when I went down to
breakfast the day after the Day of Waffles (as I will now
always remember it). For the rest of the Day of Waffles

I had floated around on a happy, sugary cloud, so perhaps Charlotte's rejection of me had begun then and I had just simply ignored it. We'd shared no classes for the rest of the day, and at lunch time, I encountered Claudia outside the music room and we stayed there, on the steps, talking about waffles and music. Claudia did not like the same singers as Charlotte. She said she preferred music that was "alternative". When she asked what I liked, I replied that I liked folk music, as I had a vague recollection of banjos and violins. 'Oh, you mean like Bob Dylan?' she said. I nodded, since it was less embarrassing to lie than have to look a fool once more for not knowing.

I enjoyed talking to Claudia. She wasn't as fun and silly as Rhiannah and her friends, but she was amiable and kind. She made me feel welcome.

The next morning, I walked into the cafeteria alone; Rhiannah was already gone when I woke up. A note pinned to the back of our bedroom door read: 'Off for an early morning walk with H & S. See you in class later. Enjoy brekkie. Bacon and eggs. Mmmmmmmm. R.'

As I walked towards the cafeteria I was intoxicated by a heady smell of frying food. By the time I entered, my mouth had begun to water and I found myself smiling giddily. I did love breakfast.

I walked over to the cafeteria matron, Mrs Butcher, and asked for a plate.

'How would you like your eggs, dear?' she asked.

'Just there, please,' I said, pointing at the small space on my plate that wasn't taken by bacon or toast.

Mrs Butcher laughed. 'You're funny, sweetie. I meant do you want them fried, poached or scrambled?'

'Oh,' I said, feeling my face redden. I hadn't been trying to be funny. 'Fried, please,' I mumbled.

I took my tray and scanned the cafeteria for somewhere to sit. My eyes caught Charlotte's table and I began moving towards it. The girls all looked up and stared at me. Claudia smiled and I smiled back. Then I saw Inga jab Claudia in the ribs.

By the time I reached their table, I knew I had made a mistake. There was just something about their *eyes*, Connolly. And there was a smell in the air. A smell of aggression.

Still, I couldn't simply turn and walk away, so I said, 'May I sit here? Charlotte?'

Charlotte's eyes seemed paler than yesterday. Icier. 'I'm sorry,' she said. 'You made your decision. You chose those other girls. The *ferals*. You can't have it both ways.'

'Oh,' I said, because I couldn't think of anything else to say. I felt humiliated.

'You had every opportunity to do the right thing,' Inga said. 'You were lucky. Not every girl who starts here gets a free pass into our group. You had an advantage and you stuffed up. Big time.'

'We can't be seen associating with someone who also associates with *them*. It would ruin our reputations,' Amy added, a hint of a smug smile tugging her glossy lips upwards.

I looked from one girl to the next. A voice inside my head said, *Walk away. Save your energy for when the fight is worth it.*

And, I reasoned, when I have a chance of winning.

'Okay, well, enjoy your breakfast,' I said and made to walk away. A moment later I found myself hurtling forwards, eggs and juice cascading into the air and all over my uniform. Something . . . or *someone* had tripped me.

'Oops,' said Kelly, giggling. 'That really was an accident.'

Later, after mathematics class, I was leaving the room when I heard Laurel's voice call out, 'Tessa!'

'Yes?' I said, turning around to face her, expecting to see her smiling her usual daffy smile at me. Instead, her face was serious.

'Turn around,' she said. I did so, curiously. I felt a scraping sensation on my back and immediately grew fearful.

My scars.

She touched my scars.

'What are you doing?' I exclaimed, wheeling around.

My scars felt as though red hot pokers were pressed against them.

Laurel held out a small square of yellow paper. On it was the word 'Freak'.

'What . . . is it for? What does it *mean*?'

'Amy put it on your back,' Laurel sighed. 'She does that sometimes. It's stupid. She thinks it's funny. Don't worry about her. She's a stupid, giant troll, and she has pimples on her back. I saw them at swimming carnival. Come on. Let's get out of here.'

I looked behind me to Charlotte and her friends. They were all cackling as though someone had told them the funniest joke ever. Except Claudia. Claudia looked at me with an expression on her face that seemed to be a mixture of guilt and pity. But she hadn't stopped Amy, had she? She hadn't come after me and warned me.

She was scared, I realised. Scared of Charlotte. Scared of being made an outcast, like I was.

Laurel and I walked towards our lockers.

I could tell from several yards away that there was something different about my locker. Instead of the plain, shiny metal that was usually its facade, it now had slashes of bold red adorning it. My pace quickened and I soon found myself at my locker, reading the words 'Tessa Connolly is an untouchable'.

'What does that mean?' I asked Laurel.

'It means you crossed them,' she said. 'It's happened to all of us. You cross Charlotte's royal court, you're untouchable. It means none of the other girls are allowed to be friends with you.'

I remembered what Harriet had told me: *'Don't mess with the in-crowd or they will mess you back.'*

I felt tears prickle at my eyes. 'So you and Erin, and Rhiannah and Harriet and Sara . . . you won't be friends with me any more?'

Laurel finally smiled. 'Oh, no. *We* can still be mates with you,' she said. 'We're untouchables too.'

It was a comfort, Connolly, but still, I felt nauseated and guilty. I thought you would be disappointed in me. You wanted me to do well at school, and be friends with Charlotte, and I had failed.

'Come on, Tess,' said Laurel, seeing my miserable expression. 'It's not so bad. You've still got us. And you don't want to be friends with those cows anyway. They'll suck the life out of you. Stick with us freaks and you'll have a much better time.'

I smiled at Laurel. She was right. I did have a better time with her, and with Rhiannah's gang, than I had with Charlotte and her friends. Perhaps this 'untouchable' business was for the best.

'That's the spirit,' said Laurel. 'Now, come with me. I have a stash of doughnuts in my room. They cure all.'

CHAPTER

THIRTEEN

YOU DIDN'T WARN ME ABOUT THIS, CONNOLLY.

I'm not mad at you. You had so much to think about; so much to remember to tell me about that I don't blame you for forgetting this. And, besides, you probably assumed I would know.

After all, it's *my* body.

I *didn't* know, though. I didn't know that my body would do this.

We were in history – one of the classes that Rhiannah and I shared. We were learning about Tasmania in colonial times, and I had just surprised Mr Beagle (and myself), by remembering that the first name for Tasmania was Van Diemen's Land, and that the colony was named after Anthony Van Diemen, who was the Governor-

General of the Dutch East Indies. He was the one who sent the explorer, Abel Tasman, on his voyage of discovery in 1642, and so Tasman named Van Diemen's Land in his honour.

I didn't know how much my teachers had been told about my lost memory. I supposed they must have been told something, so I would not be unfairly penalised in class.

My classmates knew only that I had been through a trauma, though they didn't know the nature of it. Ms Hindmarsh and I had a long conversation about how much to tell the other students. She knew most of what had happened (the parts you and I knew, anyway), and she wanted to know how much I wanted made public.

'I think we should tell them I am an orphan and that I was in hospital,' I said, after thinking for a few moments. 'But I think I don't want them to know about my memory. And I don't want them to know I was found on the mountain, in the *condition* I was in.'

'That's probably for the best,' said Ms Hindmarsh, smiling. 'We wouldn't want the girls to panic, thinking there is an attacker out there – not that I think that's what happened to you. I just know how quickly hysteria can spread with those girls. And the parents. We don't want parents to think that this is an unsafe place to send their girls. Cascade Falls is a very safe place for girls . . .'

Ms Hindmarsh's voice trailed off and her eyes became dreamy and wistful. I thought, not for the first time, that while she seemed effervescent and jolly on the outside, there were worlds inside Ms Hindmarsh that were very well hidden.

She cleared her throat. 'I know you know about Cat Connolly,' she said. 'And while her disappearance was, oh . . . just horrible for all of us, I wouldn't want you to think that this school was at fault, Tessa. Nobody knows exactly what happened that day, but it wasn't our fault.'

I wondered who Ms Hindmarsh was trying to convince. Me or herself.

Ms Hindmarsh continued. 'I think it's a really sensible idea to tell your classmates you have been in hospital. 'It will help them understand you.'

I agreed with her. I wanted to be understood.

I had seen some of them giving me curious looks. I suppose they were wondering about the exact nature of my ordeal.

But none of them knew about my memory.

That became obvious when I answered Mr Beagle's question and none of them looked surprised or even very interested.

But Mr Beagle did. Or, at the very least, he looked *curious.*

When I found out Mr Beagle was to be my history teacher, I was somewhat anxious. I remembered his grouchiness towards Laurel and Erin on the day I arrived at Cascade Falls.

In class, he still seemed grumpy most of the time, but not so very scary.

He was still wearing the same tweed suit as far as I could tell, unless he had a wardrobe full of tweed suits, and I noticed it sagged slightly at the knees and elbows. It looked quite threadbare and, as I looked at Mr Beagle's ruddy face and tired eyes, I noticed that *he* looked a bit threadbare, too, and a bit saggy. He looked like a popped balloon, and I wondered what had been the pin that had made him deflate.

He had spent much of the lesson looking at his desk, or the book in his hand, or the floor. He looked up, briefly, when others answered his questions, but he seemed almost bored by their answers and simply nodded as acknowledgement and then returned his attention to the book. When I answered the question, however, his eyes fixed on me, and he inclined his head to one side thoughtfully. 'So you haven't . . .' he began. Then he shook his head and said, 'Well done, Tessa. Did everybody hear Tessa's answer?'

Twenty-nine girls shook their heads. Beside me, Rhiannah nodded.

I felt a warm glow knowing that Rhiannah had heard my answer; she cared enough about me to listen, when my other classmates obviously found the lesson too dull to bother.

'Tessa, can you repeat what you just said?' said Mr Beagle.

'The first name for Tasmania was –' I began.

That's when I felt it.

Between my legs. Wet and hot.

And in my belly, a pang like a branch being snapped.

'What's wrong, Tessa?' asked Mr Beagle.

'Nothing, nothing,' I said, feeling my face reddening.

'Then finish what you were saying. Go on. The first name for Tasmania was . . .'

'Van Diemen's Land. Named after Anthony van Diemen, Governor-General of the Dutch East Indies, who was the one who sent Abel Tasman, on his voyage in 1642. Mr Beagle, may I please be excused for a few moments?' I said very quickly.

Mr Beagle narrowed his eyes, and I could see his mouth starting to form the word 'no'.

'Mr Beagle, I don't think Tessa's very well.' I turned around to see Rhiannah looking at me, a concerned expression on her face. 'You know she's just been in hospital. I think she should go to the sick room. I can take her, if you like.'

'Is that true, Tessa?' asked Mr Beagle, his face turning from grouchy to something close to concern. 'You're ill?'

I nodded. 'I'm not quite . . . right,' I said, which was true.

Something was happening. And it *wasn't* quite right.

Mr Beagle rubbed at his wrinkled forehead and grumbled, 'All right, then. But, Rhiannah, I want *you* at least to be back before the end of the lesson, okay?'

Rhiannah nodded quickly and said, 'Of course, Mr Beagle.'

As we walked out, I could feel Charlotte and her friends watching me again.

I sneaked a glance at her and chanced a small smile. Her top lip curled up in a way that was definitely not smiling. Next to her, Inga rolled her eyes and whispered something in Charlotte's ear that sounded very much like, 'You were so lucky to get rid of her, Charlotte. She's a freak.'

I felt my cheeks burn with shame.

Charlotte and her friends hated me *and* they thought I was a freak. And they didn't even know everything. They didn't even know the *really* freakish parts.

A few moments later, in the corridor, Rhiannah grabbed my arm and said, 'So, what's the matter, Tessa? Are we actually going to the sick room?'

'I thought that's where you were taking me,' I replied, confused. That's where Rhiannah had just *told* Mr Beagle she was taking me.

'If that's where you *need* to go, then that's where I'm taking you,' she said. 'Do you feel a migraine coming on, or the flu or whatever?'

'The flu?'

Another word I hadn't heard before.

Rhiannah put her palm on my forehead. 'No temperature,' she said. 'Are you achy? Is your throat sore? Does your head hurt?'

I thought of my back, which was still throbbing. I didn't think that was the kind of ache that Rhiannah was talking about, and I didn't think I had any of the other symptoms, so I shook my head. 'No.'

'Then you probably don't have the flu. Worst luck for you. The flu gets you out of a whole week of school. Sometimes they even send you home, and if they don't you get total star treatment. Ice cream and soup and lemon tea delivered straight to your room. You should've got flu.'

The way Rhiannah talked about it, I almost wished I *did* have this 'flu', even though the symptoms sounded quite horrid.

If it meant ice cream.

If it meant going home, which would mean, I supposed,

going to you, Connolly, in Sandy Bay. I would still really have liked to do that.

'It's . . .' I began, and then I didn't know how to finish. My face felt all hot again. I didn't know how to tell Rhiannah that my sickness was *down there.*

'You can *tell* me, Tess!' Rhiannah said, rolling her eyes. 'Seriously, I'm the girl who had to wear an eye patch for three weeks because I got a piece of bark in my eye and it got infected and everybody called me "Jack Sparrow". Embarrassing medical complaints I can handle, okay?'

'It's . . . wetness,' I said, finally, feeling a wave of relief crash over me at having finally said it. 'Between my legs.'

'You got your period?' Rhiannah's voice was quieter now.

I didn't know what to say. Did I have my 'period'? I wasn't sure. I did not recognise the word. So I just nodded. If that was the word that Rhiannah gave to what was happening to me, then that's what was happening.

'Well, why didn't you just say so?' asked Rhiannah. Then, her eyes widened. 'It's not your first one, is it?'

I nodded. Even though I wasn't really sure. The wetness was beginning to feel familiar, but I still did not know what to do about it.

'Whoa. Okay, that's pretty late for a first period. But I guess everyone's different. Okay, no sick bay for you. Let's skedaddle to the ladies'. By an absolutely fabulous coincidence, I too am surfing the crimson wave, so I can be of assistance in the cleaning up department. What, don't look at me like that! Yuck! I mean that I have tampons. You're saved. Let's get out of here.'

Just when I thought I was finally beginning to understand this new life I found myself in!

Periods.

Crimson waves.

Tampons.

So many words I did not know.

But I trusted Rhiannah, so I said, 'Yes, please, let's go.'

cHapteR
fouRteen

Later, in our room, Rhiannah showed me the 'stockpile' of 'tampons' and 'pads' in her top drawer. Before we'd gone back to class, she'd pressed another one in my hand and instructed me to, 'Put it in your pocket. Change it in a couple of hours, okay? It's important. You'll get sick if you don't. And later we'll get you some more.'

Now, she gestured to the boxes and parcels and said, 'Feel free to just help yourself any time. I've always got a whole heap, just in case.'

'Thank you,' I replied, hoping she understood that I meant 'thank you' for more than just the items that filled her drawer.

Rhiannah had been a real friend to me, Connolly. She took me to the girls' toilets, and she sat outside while

I negotiated my way with my very first tampon. It was difficult, and it hurt at first, and I found myself yelping – from the pain and from embarrassment.

But Rhiannah never got embarrassed. Rhiannah knew just what to say, and she stayed with me until I got it right.

'It gets easier,' she said. 'In a couple of days, you won't even have to think about it.'

She never once made me feel strange or abnormal for never having done it before, or even for not *knowing* about it. It was as if she understood that the reasons were complex, and that I would tell her when I was ready.

And I knew I *would* tell her. I knew she was the right person to tell my secrets to.

Rhiannah was a real friend.

It was very nice being in our room with her, too. We did our homework together. I helped her with English, and she filled in the blanks that were in my mind in mathematics, science and history. If I didn't know something – something that might be obvious to someone who had not lost their memory – she patiently explained it to me.

When we had finished our tasks, we sat on Rhiannah's bed talking.

Well, Rhiannah talked. And I listened. And it was nice.

She told me about how her family were descended from the indigenous people of Tasmania, and how her mother and father were both environmental activists. She told me that she had grown up on the north-west coast of Tasmania, in a place called Wynyard, but now her family lived in a small house in a country town called Ranelagh, just south of Hobart. They grew vegetables to earn money, and they sold them at the weekend markets.

'I miss them heaps when I'm at school,' she said. 'But, you know, it's important that I'm here.' She didn't tell me why.

She did tell me that she had a brother who went to Valley Grammar. She said he could be a 'pain in the arse', but she was glad he was in Hobart with her.

When she mentioned his name, 'Perrin', I felt my cheeks burn. I remembered the dark-haired boy at the school gates. Deep in my pelvis, something pulsed. Angrily, I willed it away and tried to concentrate on Rhiannah's story.

As I listened, and Rhiannah's life opened up to me like a flower, I thought again of your daughter.

Rhiannah told me how she loved to bushwalk, because it was something her family used to do a lot back when she lived in Wynyard, in a very special forest called the Tarkine. She said going on bushwalks down here was different – it was a different kind of bush – but it still made her feel close to home. When she was in the bush it was the only time she felt truly herself.

It seemed like the right time to ask. 'Rhiannah?' I began, when she paused to take a sip from her water glass.

'I was wondering . . . Connolly, the policewoman who found me after my accident. She had a daughter . . .'

'Cat,' said Rhiannah, nodding.

'You knew her?' I asked.

Rhiannah sighed and rubbed at her temples. 'I was wondering when this would come up. I kind of fobbed you off yesterday, when you asked about my other roommate. I'm sorry. I just didn't know what to say and I didn't really know if I could, well, trust you.'

'Was Cat your roommate?' I asked, already knowing the answer.

Rhiannah nodded, and her dark eyes began to glimmer with tears. She cleared her throat. 'Yes,' she said. 'And my friend. I don't know what you've been told about her, Tess, but she wasn't really bad. All the stories about being a big rebel . . . I think it was just a front. An insecurity thing. She was funny and sweet, and she'd make up silly dances to cheer me up, and we'd have mini midnight parties in here, with chips and salsa, which always got all over the doonas and got us into strife with the cleaners.' She laughed, her eyes looking upwards as she recalled the happy memory. 'I didn't spend enough time with her. I wish I had. We had the best time. I really miss her.'

'Do you know what happened to her?' I asked. 'I mean, how she went missing?'

Rhiannah shook her head. 'No, not really. I mean, I have my theories, but nobody really knows. She just disappeared. I'm trying to figure it out, though.'

'Me, too,' I replied. 'I promised Connolly I would.'

Rhiannah nodded, her eyebrows furrowing. 'Okay.'

'Maybe we can do it together,' I suggested.

'I don't know if we can,' she said, shaking her head. 'I'm not sure if it's something . . . I just don't know, Tessa. It could be dangerous.'

'How?' I asked. 'Do you mean that the bush is dangerous? Because, I don't know for *sure*, but I was found in the bush, so I'm guessing I've bushwalked before.'

Rhiannah looked at me curiously, and I could tell she wanted to ask, '*How can you not know if you've bushwalked before?*'

But she didn't. Again, she gave me space and time. I knew I should give her time in return. But I promised you, Connolly, and I intended to keep that promise. Finding Cat was my purpose. I had to make progress on it, even if it meant being a bit *forceful* with Rhiannah.

'Please let me come?' I pushed.

'Okay,' she said, slowly. 'I mean, *maybe*.'

'When are you going next?'

'Tomorrow night.' And then her voice turned hard and adamant. 'But tomorrow night is not the night for you to come. It's going to be a difficult walk. When you come with me, it should be on an easier walk – just so we can assess your skills – and probably during the daytime. A night-time walk is definitely not the right kind of walk for you to start on.'

'Okay,' I said. 'Not tomorrow, then. I won't come tomorrow.'

And at the time, I meant it.

CHAPTER
fifteen

that night, there were no monsters in my dreams. There was no darkness. There was me, alone, in a sun-dappled grove, in the middle of a forest.

I was on a bushwalk. By myself. But I was not scared.

In the corner of my vision I sensed movement, then heard a small twig break. My breath quickened, but I stilled myself. I did not want to appear as though I had seen or heard.

Then, at my ear, a warm breath. 'What are you doing out here all alone, little girl?' came a whisper. My face broke into a smile, and I let him run his fingers gently down my neck, down my shoulders. I let him slide his arms around my waist.

'I love you,' he whispered as reality pulled me, dragging my heels, to wake.

CHapteR

sixteen

'THE femaLe factoRy at tHe cascaDes opeRateD between 1828 and 1856,' said Mr Beagle, reading from his notes. 'The site of the factory was originally a rum distillery, run by a company called "Lowe's". The colonial government bought the distillery in 1827. Builders – under the direction of an architect called John Lee Archer – extended the buildings that were already there in order to make enough space for the ever-increasing numbers of female convicts imprisoned in Tasmania. At its fullest, the Factory housed twelve hundred women, who were engaged . . .'

'And children,' I whispered. The words just slipped out of my mouth. I didn't know where they came from, and I did not call for them to emerge. They just did.

'Sorry, what was that, Tessa?' asked Mr Beagle, looking up from his papers. I jumped in surprise. I thought I had whispered very quietly; so quietly nobody would have been able to hear me. But Mr Beagle had.

'I . . . I said "and children", Mr Beagle,' I replied. I wriggled in my seat uncomfortably. I could feel the eyes of my classmates burning into my back and sides. 'There were children at the Factory too, weren't there?'

Even though I made it into a question, I knew it to be true.

I didn't know how I knew, though.

And I didn't know why it suddenly seemed so important to say it, and to have Mr Beagle verify it. It just was.

Mr Beagle nodded slowly. 'Well, yes, there were, Tessa. Children often stayed with their mothers, though most of them were sent away to orphanages and boarding schools. Well done.'

He began to read from his notes again, and the words washed over me. I didn't hear any of them. I could still feel everybody staring at me.

I knew they talked of me. I knew Charlotte and her friends were spreading rumours about me. Rumours that I had been in an asylum before I came to school. Rumours that I was mad and dangerous. I had only been at Cascade Falls a handful of days, yet already people were beginning to think me strange.

And I was beginning to agree with them.

In the shower that morning, as I scrubbed at my back with my flannel wash-cloth, and the soap that smelled of lemon peel and roses, I noticed that my scars seemed to have raised and hardened.

Before, they had been flat to my skin, but now they made ridges down my back, like tree roots pushing up through the dirt. The feeling made me gasp, and my eyes prickled with tears. It felt as though my body was rebelling against me. First, the 'period', and now this.

Even though the rooms of Cascade Falls seemed to swelter with an excess of heating, I put on both my uniform shirt and my thick woollen blazer. I was scared that my scars might be seen if I wore only my shirt.

I wanted to call and tell you, Connolly. It felt like you were the only person I *could* tell. But it was nearly breakfast time, and Rhiannah was expecting me. Today she was introducing me to 'muesli'.

And besides, I knew you were busy. I knew you had bigger worries than some misbehaving scars. Even if you did say to call any time. I would wait. I would wait until I had bigger news before I bothered you.

As I sat in Mr Beagle's history class, not listening as he droned on about convicts and washing rooms and George Arthur and *The Rules and Regulations for the Management of the House of Correction for Females* (all subjects about which I felt I had heard many times before – probably in other history classes before my accident), all I could think about was how hot I was in my itchy jacket and how my scars must look beneath it. I wondered if they were growing still, or if they had shrunk back down again.

Perhaps it was only the hot water that had irritated them, or the lemon peel soap.

Then Mr Beagle said something that made my brain snap to attention. I don't know which word it was that dragged me back from the depths of my mind and into the history classroom.

Perhaps it was the date, '1851', or maybe the name, 'Sir Edward Chassebury'. Or maybe it was the last word he said, the word that I understood and yet did not; the word I felt I had heard before and yet sounded like a foreign language.

'*Ipecacuanha*'.

I opened my mouth to ask him, 'What is that, Mr Beagle? What is ipecacuanha?'

The bell rang out, loud and jarring, from the black box on the wall. It made me jump, and I felt Rhiannah's hand rush to my arm.

'You okay?' she whispered.

I nodded, though my heart felt as if it would beat its way out of my chest.

At the front of the classroom, Mr Beagle said, 'Well, that's enough for today, girls. Tomorrow, we will be talking about the founding of *The Mercury* newspaper.'

When we got out of the classroom, Rhiannah grabbed my hand and said, 'You look really shaken up, Tessa. Are you sure you're okay?'

A loud voice interrupted us. 'Yo, Rin!' echoed down the hallway.

I turned around to see Harriet sprinting towards us, tall and lithe and speedy as a brumby horse. The sun that streamed through the stained glass windows bounced off the gilded streaks in her hair.

Sara followed, pushing her glasses up her nose with her finger.

'You ready for tonight?' asked Harriet, punching Rhiannah on the arm. 'You're not too *freaked out,* are you? I mean after what Perrin –'

Behind her, Sara hissed the shortest sentence I had ever heard spring from her lips. 'Harriet . . . not now . . . Tessa!'

I looked quickly at Rhiannah, who was already staring back at me, her face paler than ever. 'I told them you wanted to come,' she said, her voice smooth, contrasting with her nervous dark eyes. 'I told them I said that it would be too dangerous. Right, Harry?'

Harriet nodded quickly. 'Yeah, sorry, Tess. It's just, night-time walks can be pretty full on.'

'Was it a night-time walk when Cat went missing?' I asked.

Harriet's eyes widened. Behind her, I heard Sara make a little gasping-choking noise.

'You told her about that?' asked Harriet.

Rhiannah shrugged. 'I thought I should. She would have found out anyway, and I thought it was probably better to hear it from me. Besides, she knows Cat's mum, so . . .'

'So, was it?' I asked again. 'Was it one of the dangerous night-time walks? Was that why Cat went missing?'

Rhiannah shook her head. 'No, Tess. It wasn't. Cat went on a night-time walk the week before, but the day she went missing, it was just an ordinary day walk. A pretty cruisy one. And it was a big group one. Everybody was there. It was part of our assessment for PE, so everybody had to come. Even Charlotte and her royal court made an appearance. They hated every minute of it, but they came, and they coped. Just.'

'Do you remember how Amy got her stupid knee-high boot heel stuck in the mud?' asked Harriet, giggling.

'And Inga and Kelly and Claudia all had to pull her out, and they asked Jenna and Bridget to help them, but Bridget said "Eew, no way am I going anywhere near that", and Amy didn't speak to her for a week? It was pretty funny,' said Sara.

Rhiannah nodded and smiled, but it was obvious she wasn't thinking about Charlotte's silly friends. 'Nobody saw her wander off,' she said quietly. 'And it was a pretty safe area. The path we take for the night walks isn't far from there – just up the mountain a bit – so Cat had done that just the week before. She knew the terrain.' Rhiannah shook her head. 'But it just goes to show that even experienced bushwalkers can get into trouble, on pretty simple hikes. Tess, we'll go together one day soon. Maybe at the weekend, if you're not going off campus? I'm staying here this weekend, so that might be a good time for us to go?'

I nodded. 'Yes, thank you, Rhiannah. That sounds good.'

And I meant it. I thought it would be fun to go walking with Rhiannah at the weekend.

But I was also thinking of ways I could secretly go on the walk that night. Cat had been lost in that bush. It was possible that she may have moved on from there, but I had no other trail to follow. I did not care if I was disobeying Rhiannah's wishes. I had to go.

Just as I knew, instinctively, that Cat was alive, I also knew now that going with Rhiannah and the girls out into the bush was my best chance of finding her.

CHAPTER

seventeen

I WAS WORRIED THAT RHIANNAH WOULD NOTICE my blanket.

Since I usually slept beneath just the sheet, I was worried that she would notice that the blanket was pulled right up to my chin.

But she didn't.

She raced around the room like a possum, grabbing this and that – boots and backpack and coat and funny woollen hat and black electronic box that crackled and hummed and squealed and made her even *sound* like a possum (a *two-way*, my brain reminded me. The black box is a *two-way*) and muttering to herself about 'Strickland Falls' and 'the Rivulet Track'.

Finally, when she had all of her equipment together,

she turned and smiled and said breathlessly, 'Night, Tess. Sorry to run out on you. Feel free to use the CD player or whatever. I've mainly got Xavier Rudd and The Cat Empire, but you might like them.'

I didn't bother telling Rhiannah that I didn't know what a CD player was, or a Cat Empire, and I had never heard of a man called Xavier Rudd.

I wouldn't be needing any of that tonight. Tonight, I was going on a bushwalk.

Now, please don't be mad at me, Connolly. I know you told me to be mindful, and to look after myself, but you also told me to be brave.

I was being brave.

As soon as I heard Rhiannah's footsteps padding down the hallway and the sound of Harriet's loud voice calling, 'Hey, Rin? You ready? We're running late', I threw off my blanket and breathed a sigh of relief at the relative coolness.

It's very hot beneath a blanket when you're wearing a coat and pants and boots.

I eased myself quietly up and out of bed.

My clothing rubbed uncomfortably on my back as I moved – my scars were still raised and painful, even more painful tonight – but I ignored it.

I reached below the bed for my own equipment: a torch that I'd found in the science lab and managed to sneakily borrow (*borrow*, not steal), an apple (for sustenance), and Laurel's woollen hat.

She had looked at me curiously when I asked her for it.

I saw her walking along after class, flipping it over and over in her hand. I remembered enough from my life before to know that it is very important to keep your head warm when you are out in the elements.

So I took a big, deep breath, and told myself to be brave. 'Laurel?' I asked.

Laurel froze and turned around, her eyes wide and fearful, the breath caught in her throat. When she saw me, she breathed out heavily and her muscles relaxed. 'Tessa!' she said, smiling. 'You scared the crap out of me. I didn't recognise your voice at first, and I thought you were a teacher.' She leaned in close to my ear and whispered, 'And usually when a teacher is calling my name, it is *not* a good thing!'

She leaned back out. 'Anyway,' she said. 'What can I do you for?'

I made up a story about not feeling well and my head being cold, and asked to borrow her hat.

She hesitated for a moment, and narrowed her eyes at me, biting her lip. Then she shrugged and said, 'Sure, why not. But don't lose it. It's one of my favourites. It used to belong to my nanna, and anyway, it's ace for when the red devil isn't behaving itself.' She pointed to the curly red bonfire crackling away on her head. 'Just give it back when you're better, 'kay?'

I pulled the hat out now and pushed it roughly onto my head, then strode towards the door. My hand was on the doorknob, just about to turn, before I remembered.

I cursed under my breath and turned back around.

I sprinted, feet light on the carpet, to Rhiannah's top drawer, pulled it silently open, and grabbed a handful of tampons and pads. The last thing I wanted was to be alone in the wilderness and feel that wetness between my legs again.

Just as I was shutting the drawer, I noticed it.

Glinting and glimmering in the corner.

It was Rhiannah's copper bangle.

I knew I shouldn't. It was Rhiannah's private thing, in Rhiannah's private drawer, and she had asked me not to touch it, but I couldn't help it. Just as before, my fingers were drawn to it. Just as before, I imagined footprints dancing over its glinting surface. I reached further into the drawer and brushed it, just lightly, with my fingertips.

The jolt was so strong and so sudden and so sharp, I cried out with shock and pain and fell to the floor. It was like nothing I had ever felt before. It was like a million needles sticking into my fingers, like scalding water being poured over my whole hand. It hurt so much I couldn't breathe.

I looked down at my hand and was shocked to see there was no mark. No bruise. No blood. No burn.

My eyes were tingling with tears and my head was thudding.

What had just happened? What had caused that jolt, that pain?

It couldn't possibly have been Rhiannah's bangle, could it?

I didn't even bother to close the drawer. I was too scared. I just scrabbled my way to my feet and ran from the room.

It didn't take long to catch up with Rhiannah and Sara and Harriet. They were still within the school's grounds, standing in a triangle and dressed in identical black clothes and woollen hats. They weren't talking yet, but seemed to be organising their equipment: looking at maps, preparing.

Though it was dark, my eyes could make out their faces and their bodies quite clearly. It was as if I had created by some magic a daytime within the night, but only for me. I put the torch back in my bag. I did not think I would be needing it.

Though I knew it was improbable that their eyes could see as well as mine, I shrank back and sidled behind a gum tree by the entrance to the building. From there I could watch them and they would not see me.

Over the tang of eucalyptus, I could *smell* them, too. They smelled of sweet vanilla perfume and sweat and . . . *fear*. And I could hear, loudly as if my ear was pressed against their chests, the beating of their hearts; rapid like the hearts of small animals.

And it wasn't only Rhiannah and the others that I could smell, or see, or hear. I could smell each flower in the garden separately and distinctly. I could see far away to the walls of Cascade Falls; to the cracks and ridges in the stone and the sheen of the metal spikes that sat on top like enemy soldiers, bayonets in hand. I could hear every cricket singing in the grass, and every small animal scrabbling in the bushes.

And, when Harriet and Sara and Rhiannah began to talk, each word carried to me crisp and clear. For once I was grateful for my heightened senses. I knew that Charlotte and her friends would find my powers "freakish", but they were nowhere around. I enjoyed my new senses. They were useful.

'I can't wait 'til we can dump all of this crap,' Harriet said. 'Why do we have to go through this show of bringing all this stuff every time? It's not like we *need* boots or walkie-talkies.'

'Harriet, you know Ms Hindmarsh would never let us out without all this stuff,' said Rhiannah. 'Remember when I forgot my boots the other night? I was petrified she'd catch us coming back and see my bare feet and have a go at me about, you know, the stuff she always has a go at me about. Safety and the reputation of the school and blah blah blah. It's okay. We can dump it soon.'

There was silence for a moment, and then Rhiannah went on. 'Now, you know it's going to be difficult tonight,' she said. 'Perrin told me. They've upped their night-time patrols of the grounds. Obviously they think the same as Perrin does. They must think it's important to increase their forces. There are Thylas everywhere tonight.'

It felt as if my heart stopped beating for a moment. The hairs on the back of my neck stood up on end.

'*Thyla*'.

I was sure I hadn't heard that word in my new life, and yet it seemed so familiar. It must be a word from my past.

Thyla. Like 'thylacine'. Like the stained glass at Cascade Falls.

What did it mean?

And why did it move me so?

Harriet laughed, and the sound cracked through my mind like a slap. 'It really makes you wonder, doesn't it?'

she said. 'How humans could be so dumb. I mean, hello? Extinct? Yeah, right!'

'Mate, you know why the Thylas have to do that,' Rhiannah said, and her voice sounded tired and bored, as if she had said this same thing a thousand times before. 'The Diemens were always tougher on them than us.'

'Only because they were scared of us,' said Harriet, and I could hear the smug grin in her voice.

'And you *also* know that not all humans do think they're dead,' Rhiannah continued, ignoring her. 'Which is their problem.'

'Yeah, exactly!' Harriet retorted. '*Their* problem. 'Why don't we just let the Diemens get them all? I mean, it would be one less hassle for us, wouldn't it? Like tonight? It would be so much easier for us to do our job without them getting in the way. I know there's all this talk of the treaty and stuff, but I dunno. Sometimes it just feels like they're jumping the gun. And I *know* that lots of stuff is going down. Raphael disappearing and that Thyla going missing on their side and, look, I know Rha thinks that Lord is getting more powerful or whatever but really, you know, we've been perfectly fine for a really long time without cosying up to the Thylas!'

'Can we please just not talk about that tonight?' Rhiannah snapped. 'Seriously, I'm over it. It's all Perrin talks about.'

'Sorry, Rin,' said Harriet, her voice softer. She put her hand on Rhiannah's arm. 'It's just, well, it's not like the Thylas are grateful to us for helping, is it? They still try to attack us every time we come close to their territory.'

'I know,' said Rhiannah. 'But there's thousands of years of history there, like Rha tells us. You know, history *he* was there for and we weren't. I think we forget sometimes that he's not actually our blood brother. He's been around for such a long time before us and he's seen stuff. He's seen it all happening. He's lived through all those years of Sarco versus Thyla. He knows it's hard to change that. We just need to do the best we can. And you know, when you say it's their problem, it's really not just *their* problem any more, is it?'

'So you believe it?' Harriet asked, her voice suddenly wavering. 'You believe what Perrin says?'

Rhiannah shook her head. 'I don't know, but all the evidence points –'

'Guys,' Sara interrupted, stepping forward and pushing her glasses up her nose. Then she paused, pulled her glasses off and stuffed them in her pocket. 'Won't be needing them for a while,' she said.

'You don't need them *anyway*,' Harriet retorted.

'Yeah, but I used to, and people would get suspicious if I suddenly stopped wearing them. Anyway, what I was going to say was, I know you're having a big philosophical debate and all of that, and I'm really sorry to interrupt you, but somebody has to keep an eye on the time, and I guess it has to be me, because it's eleven o'clock and if we don't leave now –'

'Okay, okay,' said Rhiannah. 'Thanks, Sara.'

She turned again to Harriet, clamped a hand firmly on her shoulder and looked intently into her eyes. 'Are you with us, Harry?' she asked.

Harriet sighed, loudly. 'Yeah, of course I'm with you,' she said. 'You're my clan. It's just . . . I can almost smell them, you know?

'Me too,' said Sara, scrunching up her nose. 'Rin, do you think they're close?'

Rin shook her head. 'I can smell them too, but you know their scent lingers. They can't mask it like the Diemens can. They must have been here sometime earlier on. I've been smelling them around here heaps the past couple of days. They must be upping their patrols, like we are, and increasing their numbers. The scent would be much stronger if there was a group of them patrolling.'

'Maybe there's just one,' Harriet said, her voice shaking. 'Maybe there's just one out there, watching us.'

The girls looked around, and I was worried for a moment that they would see me. I ducked down low behind the tree.

'Harriet, your sense of smell isn't strong enough yet to detect just *one* of them. Maybe in a hundred years. Don't flatter yourself,' Rhiannah said. 'We should go.'

The three girls turned around and began sprinting towards the high, spike-topped walls. They weren't heading for the gate and the black box that lets you in and out. They were heading straight for the wall – straight for the hard, rough rocks. Maybe they couldn't see like I could. Maybe, in the dark, they couldn't tell that they were about to slam into the wall.

I nearly screamed out to them, 'No! You're going to hurt yourself!'

But then, as I gasped in awe and horror, the three girls arrived at the foot of the wall, crouched low to the ground and leapt right over the top.

CHAPTER

EIGHTEEN

I STOOD FOR WHAT FELT LIKE ETERNITY, STARING AT THE empty space left by the three girls.

It was impossible.

I hadn't seen it.

I was imagining things. It wasn't . . . it couldn't have been . . . *real*.

When I fell before, after the jolt, back in my room, I must have bumped my head. That must be it. What I had just 'seen' was not possible.

'Hey, Tessa?' The voice shocked me so much I nearly fell over. I stumbled as I turned around.

With my strange night-time vision, I could make out quite clearly the owner of the voice and the girl standing beside her.

Laurel and Erin.

They were walking towards me, hugging their woollen jumpers around themselves. On their bottom halves, they wore flannel pyjamas. Laurel's were decorated with pigs, and Erin's had hundreds of tiny yellow baby chickens. Laurel's red curls were wild and messy. As they got closer, I saw that Erin's lips were pressed back in a wicked grin and her dark eyes were sparkling.

'Whatcha doing out here?' asked Erin.

'Yeah, I thought you were sick,' Laurel said.

'I am much better,' I lied, quickly.

I wondered what Laurel and Erin had seen. I wondered how well they could see in the dark.

This was an opportunity to make sure I had simply been hallucinating. If Laurel and Erin had seen nothing, then I must have injured my head. Or I was mad.

'Did you see anything . . . *strange* just then?' I asked.

Laurel thought for a moment, a finger tapping on her chin. 'Well, we did see Inga Koch running down the hall, yelling, "Okay, who stole my L'Oréal moisturiser? Whoever it was is going to *die*"!' Laurel waggled her fingers in my face and made a voice that sounded like a witch's. Then she grinned from ear to ear as she pulled a white tube from her pocket.

The label on the tube read, 'Advanced Perfect Night Cream.'

'Why did you steal Inga's night cream?' I asked distractedly. Inside my head, the words were repeating: *You're mad, you're mad, you're mad.*

Laurel shrugged. 'Partly for you. Those girls are being total bitches to you. But mostly for fun. You should have seen her, running down the hallway with her hair all scraped back in this big pink claw grip and no makeup on!'

'Yeah, she looked like one of those photos you see in *Woman's Day*: "Stars Without Their Makeup". It was classic!' said Erin. 'Just goes to show those girls are only human once their ten centimetres of makeup come off. Which is kind of disappointing. I was sort of wishing they were covered in scales . . .'

'I might go in now,' I interrupted. I was suddenly feeling very tired, and my head was beginning to ache. I was grateful that Laurel and Erin were standing up for me (in their own peculiar way) but I needed to get away from them. I just wanted to lie down and sleep and forget about what had just happened . . . and what it might mean.

'No, hang on, love. You haven't told us why *you* are outside at 11 pm,' said Erin. 'Didn't they tell you we have a curfew?'

'If there is a curfew, then why are *you* outside now?' I retorted.

Erin rolled her eyes. 'We don't really *do* curfew,' she said. 'But if you don't do curfew, you gotta do it right. Stay safe and stay hidden. You go in, but I think we'll hang around outside for a while. It's for our own safety. You know, because we have an insane makeup-deprived ogre on our tail. Right now, she's probably rallying the troops, and there's nothing scarier than a gang of bimbos who've had their makeup stolen!'

Laurel bent over double with silent, wheezy giggles.

And I laughed too. Just a little bit. Laurel and Erin were funny.

'Are you like us?' asked Erin, while Laurel attempted to cease her giggling by pressing hard on her mouth with the palm of her hand. 'Are you a bit *rebellious* too, Tessa?'

I shook my head. 'I'm not rebellious. I just needed some air.'

'Well, that *is* disappointing,' Erin replied. 'For a minute there I thought we'd found another girl who thinks Cascade Falls is bullshit.'

I felt myself blushing at Erin's coarseness. 'Um, how do you mean?' I asked feebly, feeling foolish for my embarrassment.

'You know: stupid, posh, wanky school that gets all its money from big business capitalism and churns out girls whose only goal in life is to marry posh, wanky capitalists. You know, the sort of school where girls who are as dumb as half a chicken can get to be prefects just because of who their daddies are. That sort of thing. Bullshit,' Erin said, shrugging.

'So, why do you go here, if you feel like that?' I asked.

'Scholarships,' said Laurel and Erin at exactly the same time.

'Lord's Trust scholarships. Would you believe we're actually pretty smart when we put our minds to it?' said Laurel, tapping the side of her head. 'You know there were only a few of us who got picked to go here from Scottsdale Public. What was it, E? Five of us in the beginning? The other girls couldn't hack it, though, and they were always getting in trouble for breaking curfew and stuff. Like, you reckon we're bad, you should've met them! They were the kind of bad Cat Connolly wished she was. But they didn't do it *properly*, like we do.'

My ears pricked up at the mention of Cat, but Laurel didn't share my fascination. She went back to talking about the other girls. 'They made a big show of themselves, and drew attention to themselves,' she said, rolling her eyes. 'And they went to the same places every time they sneaked out, which is the most important thing not to do. Always keep 'em guessing. Always stay one step ahead. Then you don't get caught. I was kind of glad when they left – gave us Scottsdale girls a bad name! Anyway, so they took off, never to be heard from since.'

'They still haven't heard from them?' asked Erin.

'Yeah, but it was Kelly Jones and Sally and Heidi Pritchard, remember?' She turned to me. 'The Joneses and the Pritchards aren't, like, the best of families, if you know what I mean. They're kind of rough, and there're heaps of kids in both the families. Dad said Mick Jones and Graeme Pritchard both got letters from the girls saying they were heading up to the mainland. Reckons Mick and Graeme were just happy to have the extra kids off their hands.'

'Our parents aren't like that,' said Laurel. 'Well, apart from your dad and his tigers.'

'Your father has tigers?' I asked Erin, my eyes wide. She laughed.

'Nah, mate. Not real tigers. Tassie tigers. He reckons he sees 'em sometimes, even though they're extinct. Reckons it's only white men who think they're extinct 'cos they're not in touch with nature like we are. He used to come home all freaked out from the bush and talk about seeing tigers, big as men, running around. Yeah, I know. Completely bonkers. I think he's getting better, though. He hasn't "seen one" since right before I came to Cascade Falls – not that he's told me about, anyway. Hey, actually, the last time he saw one was with Mick Jones and Graeme and your dad, remember?' she said to Laurel. 'Isn't it funny that we ended up being the kids who got sent here?'

Laurel laughed. 'Mr Lord probably reckoned he was doing us a favour, 'cos our parents were so barmy. My dad reckons he never really saw one, though. He was just backing up your dad 'cos they're mates. Our parents are all Van Diemen Industries labourers,' she explained. 'But most of the parents in Scottsdale are. Mr Lord picked us because we're super-smart. Kelly and Heidi actually were as well. They just didn't "apply" themselves like we do. We got those scholarships 'cos our dads were VDI and 'cos we're young Einsteins. End of story. And we're doing the families proud, aren't we, E? Our parents have big dreams about us being the first in our families to go to uni and then becoming lawyers and doctors. Never mind the fact that I actually want to be in a rock band.'

'And I would rather die than be a lawyer,' added Erin. 'I'm going to be a comic book artist. And you don't need a diploma from Cascade Falls to be one of those. What are you gonna be when you finish school, Tessa?'

I shook my head. I didn't know. I didn't know what I was *now*, let alone what I would be when I was older.

I was Tessa. I was tough. I was brave. I liked waffles. That was all I knew.

My voice didn't listen to my brain, though, because it suddenly blurted out, 'I will be the leader.'

'*A* leader, you mean?' asked Laurel. 'Like, the Prime Minister?'

'Yeah, I can see it,' said Erin, nodding. 'Tessa Connolly. Australia's second female Prime Minister.'

'Or third or fourth,' Laurel retorted. 'I reckon now they've seen a chick can do it just as well – better – than a bloke, they're never gonna let a bloke do it again.'

Prime Minister? Australia had a Prime Minister? And it was a woman? That all seemed very strange to me, but I resolved to find out more about it when my head did not feel as though it were about to collapse in upon itself. Besides, they were wrong. I did not mean *the* leader. I just meant leader of . . . of . . .

I sighed. I couldn't think. My brain was too befuddled. 'I need to go back to my room now,' I said.

'Okay, see ya,' said Erin, looking at me curiously.

'I'm just tired,' I added.

'No worries,' said Laurel.

As I walked away, Erin called out, 'Hey, Tessa. If you want to be a leader, do it! Don't let anything get in your way.'

'Thanks,' I called back.

'And Tessa, one more thing!' Laurel yelled.

'What?' I asked.

'If you're feeling better, can I've my hat back?' she called.

I reached in my bag and pulled out Laurel's woollen beanie, the beanie I never got to wear.

Because I can't leap walls.

I flung it over to her and it whacked Laurel in the face with an audible *thwap*.

'Ow!' she exclaimed, but she was giggling, and I don't know how a woollen hat could really have hurt her. 'You should join the softball team, with an arm like that.'

She looked down at the hat and screwed up her nose, then threw it back to me. I caught it with one hand.

'You don't want it back?' I asked.

'Nah, don't worry about it,' said Laurel. 'You might need it again. Next time you break curfew.'

'Thanks,' I said again.

I wondered when that time would be. Would I get another chance to follow Rhiannah and Harriet and Sara? Or a chance to learn more about the bushwalk that took Cat.

As I reached the door of Cascade Falls, I looked back at Laurel and Erin, and then up at the moon. It was nearly full – just a fingernail sliver away from perfect roundness.

I walked softly down the hallway and opened the door to Casa Rhiannah Tessa. The first thing I noticed was Rhiannah's open drawer. I closed it gingerly, then I changed into my pyjamas and lay down on my bed.

My head was brimming with images of girls leaping over walls.

I closed my eyes.

I knew I would not sleep.

chapter

nineteen

I was still awake when Rhiannah came in.

She opened the door with a soft click and padded barefoot over to her bed, boots in hand. She sat down and quietly pulled her top drawer open. I knew without looking what she was reaching for. The metal tapped against the side of the drawer, and then I heard a faint rubbing noise as she pushed the bangle back on her wrist.

I remembered the jolt that the bangle had given me. It didn't seem to be doing the same thing to her. If it was, she was being very brave and quiet.

I opened my eyes, just a crack, to look at Rhiannah, who stood in a shaft of moonlight.

What I saw made a scream catch in my throat.

It *was* Rhiannah I was looking at – definitely. She had

the same cuttlefish-white skin, the same ink-black hair, many of the features of her face were the same . . .

But in her mouth, I saw the hint of pointed fangs.

And her wide eyes, which were normally dark brown, were now as black as her hair, and wider and narrower. There were black markings around her nose, and her nostrils seemed to point forwards, rather than down.

The hands that were slowly, quietly, pulling down her dark trousers now no longer had slightly pointed fingernails, but long dark claws.

But it was her legs that scared me the most.

As she pulled down her jeans, I saw that the skin on her legs was mottled – white and black together. And her knees . . .

Her knees no longer pointed forwards, the way human knees did. Instead, her legs were bent backwards like an animal's. It was almost as though Rhiannah was something halfway between an animal and a human.

But then, as I watched, her knees clicked forwards, into normal, human knees. I heard her gasp quietly. Her body shuddered as the claws retracted into fingernails. I looked up to see her face jolt and shift – her ears slid sideways and her fangs flattened into regular teeth.

I squeezed my eyes tightly shut.

It's just a dream, I told myself. *It's just a dream.*

But I knew I wasn't sleeping.

CHAPTER
twenty

'Wake up, sleepyhead,' a slightly scratchy-sounding voice whispered in my ear. I felt a hand gently shaking my shoulder.

I jerked out of a brief, dreamless sleep and opened my eyes. It felt as if my eyelids were filled with glass shards.

Rhiannah was staring at me, her own eyes bloodshot, with dark half-circles tattooed beneath them.

But her irises were brown.

Definitely brown.

I wondered again if I had dreamed what I saw. Rhiannah looked normal now. Tired, but normal.

It had felt so *real*. All of it – the shock from the bangle, watching Rhiannah and the others leap over the fence, and then seeing Rhiannah *transform* when she returned.

And yet now she just looked like Rhiannah. *Had I imagined it? Was I mad?*

'How did you sleep, mate?' she asked. 'Gawd, you look as tired as I feel!'

'I feel as tired as you look,' I admitted, cringing as I felt that the broken glass was not only on my eyelids, but in my throat as well.

'Up all night studying?' she asked, indicating with her head at the pile of schoolbooks beside my bed, the ones I had been reading to try and bore myself into sleep. No matter how I tried, I simply could not find mathematics interesting. History fascinated me. Art class was exciting and fun. Science intrigued and terrified me in equal parts (we were shown photos of ears growing on mice! And men *walking on the moon*!), but mathematics I found interminably dull.

'Something like that,' I replied, and it came out like a sigh.

'Maths,' she said, rolling her eyes. 'I would've thought that'd be enough to put anybody to sleep, not keep them awake.'

'You don't like maths either?' I asked.

'Our kind usually don't,' she said, rubbing her forehead.

'What do you mean "your kind"?' I blurted.

Her head snapped up. 'I just mean . . . arty types, I guess,' she said. Her brow was furrowed and her eyes looked uneasy. 'I mean, like us. You and me. People who are more into passion and creativity than logic. I thought you were into art and writing and stuff, too.'

'I am,' I said.

'So, that's all I meant,' she said, shrugging. 'Just "our *arty* kind". That's all.'

'How was your night?' I asked, changing the subject. 'How was your bushwalk?'

Rhiannah shrugged again. 'Okay, I guess,' she said, her voice short and tense. She breathed out shakily. 'Sorry, Tessa. I know I'm snapping. I just didn't get that much sleep last night and the bushwalk . . . um, it was just long and there were, um, some other bushwalkers in our territory. They kind of got in the way. So, all in all, I'm a bit grumpy.'

'Who were the other bushwalkers?' I asked.

'Just some other people. People who are trying to, well, to do the right thing, I guess,' she said, shrugging. 'And we should probably, you know, be grateful and friendly or whatever, but it's hard because, it's like, it's *our* bushwalking territory, you know?'

'But how can that bush be *your* territory?' I asked. Rhiannah looked really uncomfortable. 'Sorry,' I said. I knew I was asking too many questions. I knew I was doing the exact thing I had been grateful to Rhiannah for *not* doing to me. I was prying. She had been so good in letting me tell her my secrets in my own time, and now I was trying to claw hers out of her by force.

Claw.

The word reminded me of what I had seen last night, attached to Rhiannah's pale hands.

Claws.

I looked down at Rhiannah's fingers now. Her nails were chipped and there was a deep scratch on her right hand. On the left one, the knuckles were black with bruises.

'Did you fall?' I asked.

Rhiannah followed my eyes down to her hands. 'Something like that,' she said, echoing my phrase from just a few moments ago.

'Do you need to talk about it?' I asked.

She shook her head. 'No,' she said, quickly. 'No, it's fine. It's complicated. Don't worry about it.' Rhiannah bit her lip and rubbed absently at the bruises on her hand.

I swallowed hard and tried to forget what I had seen or imagined the night before, and remember the good, kind Rhiannah, who had made me feel so welcome at Cascade Falls. I tried to think of the Rhiannah who was in front of me now, looking so upset.

I decided to stop my questioning. I would show Rhiannah the same respect she had shown me. 'You can tell me anything,' I said. 'But you don't have to.'

'Thanks,' she said, forcing a small smile. 'I might take you up on that one day. Maybe you can do the same.'

I nodded. 'In the meantime . . . waffles?' I asked.

Rhiannah shook her head. 'No, ma'am. Today isn't waffle day, Miss Tessa. Today is *hash brown* day!'

I had no idea what a hash brown was, but Rhiannah seemed excited by it, just as she had been about waffles. Which could only mean that hash browns were something to look forward to. I grinned right back at her and used a phrase I had heard you and Vinnie use when you were talking about your first morning coffees. I said, 'Bring it on then, Rhiannah. Hit me up with some hash browns!'

cHapteR
twenty-one

'aH, RHIANNAH! JUST tHe PeRsoN I was afteR!'

Ms Hindmarsh poked her head around the door of her office as Rhiannah and I walked back from our breakfast (which was, predictably, wondrously divine, and of which I had partaken, well, at least *one* too many 'browns'. I *was* going to get fat at this rate).

'Um, why?' Rhiannah answered, nervously.

'Nothing to worry about!' said Ms Hindmarsh, smiling. 'I just wanted a chat. Would you mind waiting here for a moment? I just need to send a quick email first. It won't take long.'

'Sure,' said Rhiannah.

'Hi, Tessa,' said Ms Hindmarsh, turning to me. 'How's everything going?'

'Really well, thank you, Ms Hindmarsh,' I said.

'Excellent,' she said, her blonde curls bobbing as she nodded. She turned back to Rhiannah. 'I won't be long, Rhiannah. I promise I won't make you late to class.'

She stuck her head back inside the door and said, 'Perrin, thank you for your time. Rhiannah's here. I'll have a chat to her on her own in a moment, if that's okay with you.'

The boy from my first day – Perrin, Rhiannah's brother – moved past Ms Hindmarsh into the hallway. Immediately, his eyes found mine, and then they scanned over me like a searchlight. I felt my skin prickle.

I liked the boy's eyes.

I liked his strong, broad chin too, and the way his slicked-back hair showed a hairline that lowered in the middle at the front in a sharp point. I liked the jagged angles of his face. I even liked the small, zigzagging scar beneath his left eye. It was the only thing about him that seemed less than perfectly beautiful, and I think it was the thing I liked best of all.

My thoughts shunted to my own appearance, the one I had seen earlier that morning in the washroom mirror. I remembered the messy crop of hay-coloured hair, the heavy-looking bags beneath my eyes, the pointy nose and too-wide mouth. I wanted to cover my face with my hands so the beautiful boy could not see how plain I was.

I wanted – for a moment – to look like Charlotte Lord, with her sleek blonde hair and perfect face. A lady's face.

Out of the fog inside my mind came a reflection of a younger me, with flowing, wavy hair, and a long pretty dress. I wished I had that dress now. I wished I had that hair.

It was the first time since my accident that I had thought anything of my appearance; the first time I had minded my boyish crop and tired features. It was the first time I had remembered the way my old self looked. Now I yearned to look like a lady. I wished to be elegant and comely. All for this boy. I wanted this boy to notice me and to think me pretty.

I knew that he would not think me pretty as I was.

Still, he was kind. He reached out and took my hand in his. 'Tessa,' he said gently, and I felt proud that Rhiannah had mentioned me. Then I wondered what else she had told him. I wondered if she'd told him about my memory.

I couldn't help noticing that he had a copper bangle too. It jumped and jiggled as he shook my hand up and down, and my eyes scanned it for signs of dancing paw prints. But it moved too fast. He opened his mouth to say something else, but before he could, Rhiannah strode between us, forcing the boy's hand to slip from mine, and said angrily, 'Perrin, what are you doing here?'

Perrin shoved his hand in his trouser pocket. The bangle was gone. 'I just came in to make sure it was okay with Ms Hindmarsh for you to go on that big bushwalk,' Perrin said. 'You remember the one?'

'And I said it was fine,' said Ms Hindmarsh, returning from her office. 'You know we're very proud of how you conduct yourself on those walks. And we would never dream of keeping you chained up behind these walls. I just want to check a few things with you, though. Where you will be walking to, that sort of thing, so if anything does go wrong we'll know where to find you. Would you mind giving me a few moments now?'

'No, Ms Hindmarsh,' said Rhiannah. She turned to me. 'You okay to get to class, mate?'

I nodded.

'Okay, well . . .' Rhiannah looked from Perrin to me and said, 'Perrin, this is Tessa. Tessa, this is Perrin. Perrin, you can go home now.'

Perrin smirked and said, 'Well, I think, sadly, I'll go back to school. Maths is up first, though, so I might drag it out here for as long as possible. I have a note that says I don't need to be in until recess time.'

'Rhiannah, now please,' said Ms Hindmarsh.

'Seeya, Tess,' said Rhiannah. 'Perrin, don't be annoying, okay?'

'Yes, sir,' Perrin drawled as Rhiannah followed Ms Hindmarsh into her office.

I turned back to her brother, feeling my stomach twist. I could not identify the feeling. Embarrassment? Anxiety? Shyness? I wasn't sure. I was torn between wanting to chat wittily with him – to be funny and pleasing and elegant – and wanting to run as quickly as I could in the opposite direction without saying a word.

Perrin just stared right back at me, the corners of his mouth turned upwards, his eyes glinting and sparkling.

He knew exactly how I was feeling.

He thought it was funny.

For some reason, this made me a little bit angry, and the anger made me forget, momentarily, about my shyness.

'What is amusing?' I asked.

'Nothing!' he said, shaking his head, his lips twitching. 'Just that . . . well, you've got that *look,*' he said. The little bit of anger had now turned into a very big bit. How did this stranger know about my *looks*? How presumptuous of him! 'That "I'm mad with Perrin" look,' he added. 'It's cute but definitely not funny.'

Despite his words, his lips were now twitching uncontrollably.

'No, you're right. It's not funny,' I snapped.

'Just a little bit?' he asked.

'You know, it is the height of impoliteness to make fun of a lady in this manner!' I retorted. It felt like a phrase I had been instructed to say. Or perhaps I read it in a book. I enjoyed saying it. I felt as if I had been longing to use those words.

My pleasure gave way as the twitch in Perrin's lips escalated into a wide and unashamed grin. 'A lady?' he said. 'Right. *Lady Tessa*. Is that what you think you are?'

I was furious now. What did *he* know? I *might* have been a lady.

'Cad!' I growled.

'Fiery,' he whispered. 'Good to see you fiery.'

'What?' I asked. 'What are you talking about? I don't even *know* you!'

A shadow passed over Perrin's face.

'You don't . . . look, forget it, okay? Forget I said anything.' He cleared his throat. 'Hey, I don't think we got the chance to shake hands properly before, because my rude little sister got in the way.' He was smiling again now.

'I don't want to shake hands with you,' I said, but a voice in my head said, *Yes you do. You want to hold his hand. You want to hold* him. To shoo away the unruly, unbidden thought, I focused on being angry. 'I think *you're* very rude,' I said. 'To laugh at me like that. And to *presume* things about me.'

Perrin shrugged. 'Maybe you just need to remember how to harden up, little girl,' he said, winking. 'Now, if you don't mind, I really do need to scram. School awaits, worst luck. I hope I'll see you again, though.'

'If you're *lucky*,' I bit back.

I turned on my heel and began marching away. It took me a few moments to realise I was marching in completely the wrong direction.

Feeling my stomach churning and the heat blazing in my face again, I stopped and turned around.

Head down, I marched back past Perrin, who was standing, arms crossed, one eyebrow raised. His lips were doing that twitching thing again. Most ungentlemanly.

'Missed me already?' he asked.

'No, Perrin,' I growled as I walked past. 'I just wanted to make sure I remembered your face, so I could run the other way next time I saw it.'

I knew it sounded spiteful and unladylike, but I also knew that I should not put up with his rudeness. He should know better than that. He needed to be reprimanded.

'That's it, little girl. That's what I mean by hardening up. Go, Tessa!'

My face flamed. I hid it and kept walking. 'Goodbye Perrin,' I muttered.

What sort of a name was 'Perrin', anyway? It sounded like a kind of baby bird, not a name for a strapping youth.

It was only when I was had walked a hundred steps away from Perrin, into the hallway that led to Mr Beagle's history classroom, that I remembered what Rhiannah had said the night before.

'*Now, you know it's going to be difficult tonight,*' she said. '*Perrin told me. They've upped their night-time patrols of the grounds. Obviously they think the same as Perrin does. They must think it's important to increase their forces. There are Thylas everywhere tonight.*'

Perrin told her.

That's what she said.

Perrin was involved in the same strangeness that Rhiannah and her friends had talked of and *created* last night in the moonlight. Yet again, the image of Rhiannah with claws and fangs burst into my mind. But it had been a dream. Just a dream. There were no strange creatures. Perrin wasn't one of them.

You're just tired, I told myself, as I slid into my usual seat, ignoring the words written in blood-red ink on the lip of my desk. 'Tessa is a freak' they said. 'You're probably right,' I whispered at the desk. Certainly, nobody normal would have such queer imaginings.

'Good morning, class,' said Mr Beagle. 'Today, we will be learning all about Sir John and Lady Jane Franklin, two of the early pioneers of Tasmania . . .'

I let his voice mute slightly in my head. I already knew

all about Sir John and Lady Jane (though, as with most
of the people, places and dates I already knew before Mr
Beagle told us, I didn't know why), so I allowed my mind
to drift away.

Back to last night.

Back to what Rhiannah had said.

Back to when she mentioned Perrin.

And back to that word she used: *Thyla*.

As I thought of it again, my scars prickled and twanged
and the pain was so great, I felt I might cry out.

But I didn't. I held it all inside as tears burned my eyes,
and I wondered again on that word. I felt as though it was
the key to some mystery. The key to Cat's disappearance,
perhaps.

Or the key to my past.

CHAPTER
twenty-two

THE PERSON I LEAST WANTED TO SEE MY SCARS WAS THE one who saw them first.

I was in the washroom at recess time, after a science lesson where I had listened to perhaps one half of what our teacher, Mrs Bush, had told us.

We were learning about the phases of the moon, in preparation for an upcoming class astronomy session. At first, I was enthralled by her words. As Mrs Bush talked about the orbits of the sun and earth, and illuminations and eclipses, my skin itched and tingled with excitement. When she told us that the astronomy session would involve a viewing of the full moon – the most famous and magical of the lunar phases – my ears began to buzz.

As she said, 'It will be an excellent opportunity for us to observe the full moon, in all its glory, with our new telescope, which was kindly provided to us by Mr Lord . . .' my scars began to throb.

It was my scars that drew my attention away from what Mrs Bush was saying. Though I was still intrigued by this talk of the moon and its powers, the pain in my scars overwhelmed me. They ached and burned and pounded – it felt as though they were coming alive and raising up even more beneath my school shirt. I was very glad I had decided to wear my thick blazer again that day.

I dimly heard the discussion turn to werewolves and contacting spirits. I wanted to listen but my scars hurt so much now it was impossible to concentrate. I closed my eyes and allowed my mind to drift away to other things.

Like Perrin.

I could see his face in my mind, with its strong angles, its white skin, its huge, dark eyes and the jagged scar that slashed across his cheek. I could see his wide, wicked grin, and his sleek, slicked-back hair. I could see the tenseness of his muscles beneath his shirt, and his strong, pale hands.

And I felt quite embarrassed about how I had acted. He wasn't really *that* rude to me, and *I* had behaved like a banshee.

I wished I could take it back. I wished I had taken his hand. Though I did not know why, I believed that holding Perrin's hand would be . . . *thrilling*.

All the while, as I thought of this, the pain in my scars grew more and more intense, until it felt as though I might faint and slide from my chair. I gripped the side of my desk to keep myself from slipping away.

Laurel, who sat next to me in science class, turned to me and whispered, 'You okay? You look kinda funny.'

'Miss Simpson, would you like to share your message with the whole class?' Mrs Bush growled, making Laurel and I both sit bolt upright.

Laurel shook her head, her fuzzy red curls bobbing and shimmying. 'Um, not really, Mrs Bush,' she replied. 'Sorry.'

'What about you, Miss Connolly?' asked Mrs Bush, and I felt a tiny blush of happiness at hearing my own name attached to yours. It felt nice, even as I was being chastised. It felt as though we were connected.

'Laurel was just asking if I was okay, Mrs Bush,' I admitted, feeling the need to stand up for Laurel. She looked across at me, gratefully. 'She was just being a good friend.'

Mrs Bush nodded, and gave a half-smile. 'I'm glad to hear it,' she said. 'I'll be even more glad if Miss Simpson can tell us the name of the "werewolf" illness I was just telling you about – the one that is connected with the full moon.'

'Lycanthropy,' I answered, before Laurel could even open her mouth (and I suspect that if she did open her mouth, she would not have given the same answer). I didn't mean to speak out of turn, and I'm not quite sure where the word sprang from. I couldn't remember hearing Mrs Bush say it.

I could tell by the look on Mrs Bush's face that she was less impressed with my answering than she was annoyed at the fact I had answered in Laurel's place.

'Sorry, Mrs Bush,' I said, quickly. 'I know you asked Laurel, but I'm really not feeling well.'

'Do you need to go to the sick room, Tessa?' asked Mrs Bush.

My scars gave another twang and I nodded.

'Okay, then. There's only five minutes or so left of class, so you may go. Have a good read of the symptoms and folklore of lycanthropy as your homework tonight, and also their basis in science, ready to give me a full report tomorrow. I hope you feel better.'

'Thanks, Mrs Bush,' I replied. I gathered up my books and left the classroom, giving Laurel a grateful smile as I walked past. She grinned back.

'Miss Simpson, focus, please,' said Mrs Bush, and I saw Laurel roll her eyes and slump further down in her seat.

By the time I left the classroom, I had already decided I would *not* go to the sick room. I had been lucky to avoid it the day of the 'period'. I knew that the nurses there already knew about me. You had asked Ms Hindmarsh to inform them so that if I did need medical attention, they would be, as you said, 'up to speed'. I wasn't afraid to tell the nurses about my scars. I was afraid that there might be some other student there in the sick room as well: one who might overhear our conversation, or catch a glimpse of my back as I showed the nurse.

I decided instead to go straight to the washroom and have a look at my scars myself, to see if they really were growing. Everyone else would still be in the classrooms. I would be alone. It would be the perfect time for me to examine my back in private.

I shrugged my thick wool blazer from my shoulders, enjoying the rush of cool air that took its place. I really could not understand how all the other girls endured the shirts and blazers – and sometimes even jumpers as well – every day. They all complained that it was cold, that winter in Hobart was torture.

I liked the cold. It made me feel alive. Being stuck inside, in the cloying, stifling heat made me feel as if I was slowly suffocating.

It was better in the washroom, though, which (when there were no running showers filling the room with steam) was the coolest place in the school. And it was better with my heavy clothes off.

After my blazer, I removed my shirt. Then I unhooked my bra (a contraption I hated, but which you said I must wear to avoid pain when running or playing sport. I did try physical education without it one day. You were right.).

I kicked off my shoes and peeled off my socks. The feeling of the cool tiles against the soles of my feet was Heaven. I padded slowly over to the mirror and, just as slowly, turned around.

What I saw made me gasp, made my face burn, made my heart flutter like the wings of a thornbill.

My scars *had* changed. Back at the hospital, when I had first been shown them, the scars had been pale pink lines across my back. They had been thick and long, and had looked as though whatever caused them had been painful – but they had just looked like scars.

Now they weren't pink any more. They were black.

And they were much thicker and wider, and raised about half a centimetre from the rest of my skin. They didn't look like scars any more.

They looked like stripes.

But still the sight of them didn't scare me. Not after I got over the first shock. In fact, they looked to me almost . . . beautiful.

I ran my hands over them, letting my fingertips ride over the bumps and ridges. It felt good. The fine hairs on my back stood up as my skin goosebumped with pleasure. My stripes liked to be touched. I smiled. Though I should have been afraid or worried for my health, I wasn't. In the cool silence of the washroom, with my fingers caressing my transformed scars, I felt sublimely happy.

The silence, and my joy, was shattered in an instant by the sound of a strangled scream.

I whirled around.

And found myself face to face with Charlotte Lord.

cHapter
twenty-tHRee

cHaRLotte LoRd HaD many fRienDs. fRienDs sHe enjoyed gossiping with. Friends she enjoyed telling secrets to.

And Charlotte Lord's friends liked gossiping too.

By the end of the day, I felt every eye in Cascade Falls upon me, and I heard my name whispered behind every mouth-shielding hand.

Everyone knew. They knew I wasn't normal. They knew I was *different*. And it hurt. It hurt so badly.

I limped my way through afternoon classes, barely hearing a word any of my teachers said. My mind was full of one word only: the word that Charlotte had spat once she had finished screaming, and before she had turned and run from the washroom. The same word that Inga had used and that had been inked on my history class desk.

Freak.

That's what I was. I was a freak.

I was a girl with no memory, who had been discovered as a wild thing in the middle of the bush, who had strange dreams, who smelled more keenly, heard more powerfully, who had strength that seemed unnatural, who hated the heat that everyone else loved.

And I had stripes.

At the end of my last class – mathematics – I grabbed my books hastily and ran from the classroom as fast as I could. All I wanted was to be in my bedroom. Alone. Away from the whispers and the stares. I wanted to curl up beneath my doona and make it all go away.

As I ran down the hallway, I passed Erin and Laurel.

'Hey, Tessa! What's wrong?' Laurel called out. I shook my head and kept running. I ran all the way back to room 36. I wrenched the door open, leapt inside and shut it quickly behind me. On the other side, I turned my back to the door and slid down onto the floor. I put my head in my hands and cried.

'Tessa? What's happened?'

The voice made my head jerk upwards.

Rhiannah was lying on her bed facing me, a pile of books beside her. Her eyes were wide with concern.

'What are you doing here?' I asked, between my sobbing. 'Class only just finished.'

'I got the day off. Told Ms Hindmarsh I felt a wog coming on and I wanted to recover before the walk. I'm not really sick. I just wanted some R and R and I kind of needed to catch up on my homework. Been spending a bit too much time bushwalking lately, I guess! I found something, actually, when I was researching for history. Something kind of creepy, in an old book in the library. I think you should look at it. But do you wanna tell me what's wrong first, Tess?'

I decided it was time. Time to tell her everything.

I just needed to tell *somebody*. I mean, I know that *you* knew, Connolly, but I needed to tell someone else. Someone my own age. Someone at Cascade Falls. I banished all thoughts of bent-back legs, of leaping over walls. Rhiannah was a young girl, just like me. She was my friend. And she was strange, as I was. She would understand.

And so I told her everything. About having no memory, no past, no family. About how I was found on the mountain.

And then, finally, about my stripes.

When I told her the last part, her face grew even paler than usual, and I noticed her hands gripping the corner of the bed, her long nails digging in.

'Can I see them?' she whispered.

I shrugged. Why not? I had already told her everything. I might as well *show* her as well. I pulled my shirt up and turned around.

Rhiannah gasped. 'Oh, crap,' she whispered.

'I know. I know. I'm a freak,' I said, sniffing.

'No,' Rhiannah replied, and her voice was firm. 'No, mate. You're not. You're . . .'

Rhiannah shook her head, and stood up quickly.

'I have to go,' she said, and grabbed her backpack. She started stuffing things into it – clothing, a torch, a woollen hat.

'Where are you going?' I asked. 'Can't you stay and talk to me?'

Rhiannah shook her head quickly. 'I need to go and . . .'

She stopped and looked at me intently. Her eyes darted towards the heavy book that was on the top of the pile she had been reading. She marched over to the bed and grabbed it.

'Look at this,' she said, handing it to me. 'I found it kind of fallen down behind the library shelves. I've been trying to make sense of it all afternoon. I thought it was just a creepy coincidence, but now, after what you've shown me, maybe it makes more sense. I don't know. Just read it. I'll be back in the morning.'

'You're going out tonight?' I asked.

Rhiannah nodded. 'Yeah. Bushwalk. I'll see you tomorrow, okay?'

She raced from the room before I had time to say another word, leaving me alone with the hefty book.

My eyes brimming with tears, I looked down at it.

At first I wasn't sure what I was looking at. I wiped crossly at my eyes.

'I don't cry,' I muttered, through clenched teeth. 'I don't . . .'

As the words and pictures on the page became clearer, they sucked all the words from my throat.

I sat, open-mouthed, staring and reading and trying to make sense of what I was seeing. Finally, as I reached the end, I used a phrase I sometimes heard you use, Connolly, when you got particularly annoyed with Vinnie's grumpiness, or when some new lead about who I might be failed to produce any answers.

I let the heavy book fall with a thud to the floor, and I whispered, 'Holy hell.'

cHapter

twenty-four

THIS IS THE POINT WHERE YOU REJOIN THE STORY, Connolly. Do you remember?

It was morning when I called you. Rhiannah had not returned that night at all and, first thing the next morning, I walked to the office in my pyjamas. I told Ms Hindmarsh I was sick – that I had caught the same sickness that Rhiannah had. I said I did not think I was well enough for lessons that day, and I asked to call you.

You came straight away, like you said you would.

When I told Ms Hindmarsh I wasn't well, she looked at me curiously, and I wondered if she had heard about Charlotte and me and the washroom and my stripes.

I didn't have time to think about it. I didn't have room in my brain to think about it. I just needed you, Connolly.

I needed you to come and to look at the book and to tell me that I wasn't dreaming. I had seen so many things in the past few days that had seemed like a dream; that had seemed so unreal that I thought I must have been imagining them. I needed you – with your policewoman's logic – to tell me this was real.

'Tess!' you called out as you knocked on my door. 'Tess, it's me. Connolly.'

I raced to the door and yanked it open.

You looked tired and you looked worried, but you looked like . . . *you*.

I flung my arms around you and squeezed you as tightly as I could. I needed to believe that you were really there.

'Oi, oi! Tess!' you cried out, giggling. 'Very, *very* happy to see you too, but can I have my lungs back?'

I relaxed my grip a little bit, but I kept on hugging. I honestly didn't feel like I was capable of letting you go.

'I'm so glad you're here,' I said, feeling more unwanted, unruly tears springing to my eyes. 'I'm so, so glad you're here.'

'What's up, Tess?' you said, pulling away slightly so you could look at me. 'I mean, I figured everything was going okay. You hadn't called, so I guessed that meant you were just having too much fun.'

I sighed. 'Come inside, please,' I said, grabbing you by the hand and pulling you into room 36.

'Your roomie's not here?' you asked, looking around.

I shook my head. 'She's gone on another bushwalk,' I replied.

Your face suddenly looked pale beneath your freckles. 'Alone?' you asked.

'I'm not sure,' I said. 'Probably with our friends, Harriet and Sara.'

You looked relieved. 'Good,' you said. 'You girls should never go out into that bush alone. But, come on, Tess, I'm super curious. What have you got to tell me?'

I shook my head. 'I can't tell you, Connolly. I have to show you.'

'Okay,' you said. 'Show me.'

'I think you should sit down.'

I took you by the hand again and led you over to my bed. You sat down and I picked the book up from where I had placed it carefully on my bedside table, with a piece of card between its pages.

'Here,' I said.

You opened the book to the spot I had marked.

A few moments later, the book landed on the floor once again.

'Read it to me,' I said, once you had recovered.

'Let me hear the words. If I hear you say it, I might believe it's real.'

You looked shaky, and I could see the goosebumps that jostled with freckles for space on your arms.

You cleared your throat: once, twice –

And then you read.

'"Name: Theresa (Tessa) Geeves. Born: Hobart, Van Diemen's Land, 1836. Age: 15. Sentence: Ten years for the crime of bodily assault. Mother's place of origin: Skipton, Yorkshire." Then there is . . . there is a picture of . . . of, well, it looks like *you*, Tess,' said Connolly, looking up at me. 'But, it can't be you. You know that, don't you? I mean, this photo was taken over a hundred and fifty years ago. It might be one of your ancestors, but it can't be you.'

'Please keep reading, Connolly,' I asked. You nodded and went back to the text.

The following is a report from Female Factory guard, Isaac Livingston, on the convict Theresa Geeves, dated the first of February, 1851:

This report is compiled at the request of Female Factory Overseer, Mr Albert Hopkins, in response to the events concerning Miss Tessa Geeves. The abovementioned inmate has always been a quiet and courteous worker at the Factory, and we staff have watched her grow from a dumpling infant still in swaddling clothes, to a good, strong girl, who is brave, never cries, and is admirably keen at following instruction. It is often with a heavy heart that we farewell the children of convicts, though we know that the Factory is not a suitable place for the upbringing of young men and women. We were especially fond of young Tessa and thus it was a pleasure mixed with sadness as she joined us here again. It transpired that she had been rather too aggressive in her defence of a fellow student at the orphanage against a schoolyard bully. While her crime may, in many people's eyes, be seen as heroic, the matron of the orphanage thought it a sure sign of vicious, violent tendencies.

I tried not to grin foolishly at the word 'heroic', though it did give me some sense of pride to find my crime was an honourable one. I did not draw attention to my gallantry, though, and let you read on.

We, of course, did not believe this to be true at the time. Tessa was such a gentle child. However, in the past month, following the events of New Year's Day, we have noticed a discernible shifting in Miss Geeves' temperament. She has turned from sensible and amenable to melancholic and, at times, even disagreeable. Of course, we are all most sympathetic to the tragic situation that is Miss Geeves' burden following her mother's passing. We understand, too, that she bears a certain quantity of resentment towards the staff at the factory, due to the circumstances surrounding this sad event. Miss Geeves firmly believes that the administration of ipecacuanha and the removal of rations, coupled with her mother's poor health, was the cause of the unfortunate incident. This belief has led her to behave in a most unladylike and, at times, frightening manner. She has been observed quarrelling with other inmates, and has attempted several times to climb the walls surrounding the facility. We have also apprehended her scratching at her clothes and, on occasion, even removing her outer layers, complaining of the heat. Finally, we have observed strange physical manifestations of her new temperament; manifestations that have caused alarm amongst some factory staff.

Suddenly visible on the inmate's back are long, slash-like scars traversing the whole of the width of her torso. There seem to be in excess of ten of these scars in total. The scars were first observed by fellow inmate, Mary Absolam, on the fifteenth day of January, when the inmates were in the wash-house. Miss Absolam relayed her observations to me, and

I duly communicated the information to Mr Hopkins. Since this day, the scars have been noticed on several subsequent occasions, and it has been noted by the observers that the scars have darkened in colour and increased in size. The transformation of these scars seemed to be in direct correlation with Miss Geeves' mental state.

Miss Absolam believes these scars to be of supernatural origin. I, of course, being a man of reason, consider simply that some unfortunate accident has befallen Miss Geeves. Perhaps it is the folly of the Flash Mob. They are sneaky, sly women, always up to no good. And so, their involvement in this business is not outside the realm of possibility.

Mr Hopkins has entrusted me with keeping watch over Miss Geeves and her troubles, and I will report back on any subsequent developments. Mr Hopkins is, of course, always conscious of the Flash Mob and their influence on our young workers, and I will personally do everything in my power to prevent Miss Geeves from falling in with this unsavoury rabble.

Regards,

Isaac Livingston

You looked up at me, your forehead furrowed, and your eyes wide and fearful. I heard you swallow, loudly.

'There's more,' I said, and my voice came out like a creaking floorboard.

You nodded. 'I know, but Tessa, you don't . . .'

I shrugged and looked down at my knees. How could I explain it to you properly?

I *knew* that the girl in the report was me.

She was the girl I had remembered when I was talking to Perrin – the girl with long, wavy, dark blonde hair, a serious face, a long cotton dress. She was *me*. I remembered seeing her reflected in the mirror. I remembered brushing and braiding that long hair. I remembered that serious face.

When I read the report, none of it seemed foreign or new. It was as though I was reading my own diary or journal. It was as though I knew everything that Mr Isaac Livingston was saying. As if it was a memory. And, as you read it again to me, I could *see* the memories.

I could see the Female Factory, with its high stone walls, peaked roofs and muddy courtyards. It was the building from my dream, and it was a building from my past. It wasn't like the building you had pointed at as we drove to Cascade Falls. That building was a hollowed husk of what the Factory used to be.

I could see fat Mr Hopkins.

I could see Isaac Livingston, too. Well, *almost*. I could see his stocky silhouette, a quick flash of amber eyes.

I could hear his deep, gravelly voice.

I could see Mary Absolam, with her limp, sweaty brown hair and her always-dripping nose.

I could remember the 'Flash Mob' – an unruly group of women who refused to give up their criminal ways and incited fear in the less confident, more refined inmates. I was one of those inmates. I had an education. I had been taught to be a lady. I had arrived back at the factory in a pretty dress. They ridiculed me for this.

I remembered that my mother paid them off in rations, begging them to stay away from me.

That part wasn't in Livingston's report, but I remembered it anyway. I also remembered Livingston coming to me, the day after Sir Edward paid his visit – the day after Sir Edward did something to my mother that made her scream and rant and cry. Livingston told me that she had died from the 'medicine' they had given her to calm her, and from a lack of food.

She had given all of her rations to me and to the Flash Mob girls, and she was starving. It was a combination of starvation and the poisonous medicine – the 'ipecacuanha' – that killed her. Now I knew why that word sounded familiar when I'd heard it in Mr Beagle's class.

That's what my dream was about. It wasn't just a dream. It was a memory. It was real.

I looked up at you and you nodded. 'I know,' you said, and I realised I didn't have to explain anything. You could see it in my eyes. 'Tess, you can understand that this seems . . . bizarre,' you went on. 'But it's real to you, isn't it? You believe it.'

'I don't just believe it,' I said. 'I *remember* it.'

'Do you have . . . the scars? I mean, I *know* you have scars, but have they . . . changed?'

I pulled up my shirt and showed you my back. I heard you gasp. 'But then, Tess, it says here in the book that . . .'

I nodded. 'Read it to me,' I said.

You cleared your throat and read again:

The following is a report from Female Factory guard, Isaac Livingston, on the convict Theresa Geeves, dated the fifth of February, 1851:

It is my unhappy duty to inform the Governors, on Mr Hopkins' behalf, that Miss Tessa Geeves has escaped from the Female Factory.

Her escape followed a week of bizarre and disturbing behaviour, during which one staff member and several other inmates – including members of the Flash Mob – were physically assaulted, and during which Miss Geeves has been apprehended on several occasions leaving her dormitory after curfew.

It was during a reprimand for this last indiscretion that Miss Geeves escaped.

I was not at my post the night that Miss Geeves disappeared, and the account given to me by the duty guard – Thomas Walter – is dubious at best. Walter reported that he happened upon Miss Geeves in the exercise yard, in a state of agitation. It was well after her curfew, so it was incumbent upon him to reprimand Miss Geeves. As he did so – and hereafter his account enters the realms of fantasy and farce – Walter reports that he noticed a curious and quite startling transformation in Miss Geeves' physical appearance.

Walter is quite specific in his imaginings. He tells us that her eyes seemed to have changed from human eyes into what he could only describe as eyes of a more marsupial nature. Her teeth became elongated and 'sharp as daggers', and – most fantastical of all – he says her legs began to buckle and bend backwards. I know it sounds quite unbelievable and, in fact, it is. I have suspicions as to the sobriety of the young guard. The transformation was, quite obviously, simply a figment of his intoxicated imagination, but I will report it here as he told it, for I hope it will serve as some excuse for his lax response to Miss Geeves' escape.

What happened next, the guard says, was this: Miss Geeves (or the creature he was hallucinating Miss Geeves into), opened her mouth and let out a sound something like a scream. It was a wild sound, he says; a bestial sound. It was not the kind of sound a human being should ever make.

After Miss Geeves ceased her 'demonic howling', she turned and, on her new, back-turning legs, she galloped towards the walls and leapt right over their top.

By the time I returned to the factory, Walter had already told Mr Hopkins of his 'observations'. Though I advised Mr Hopkins that it was quite obvious the guard had turned temporarily mad, Mr Hopkins believed the best course of action was to inform Lord Chassebury of the guard's observations, and to take action to recover 'the beast' from the woodland to which she had fled.

It has now been three days since Miss Geeves' escape and, though Mr Hopkins and Lord Chassebury have both deployed many men to scour the forests that surround our Factory, she has not been recovered.

There have been reports of strange creatures sighted in the woods – mammals much larger than any we have seen already on this island. The creatures are said to walk upright instead of on all fours, and to display bizarrely human features. Those reporting these sightings claim the beasts have only been seen in glimpses caught as they race through the trees, and yet they imagine these are creatures to be feared. They describe them to be strong, fast and wild.

Chassebury's men have informed him of the discovery of these 'new mammals', and a directive has been issued that any beast captured should be culled. Chassebury has visited Mr Hopkins' office, and Mr Hopkins informed me that a bounty much higher than that paid for the thylacines will be available to anyone who can produce a skin from one of these new mammals. He said to me that these beasts represent all that England must eradicate in this new land, if it is to be transformed from a wild and corrupted place to a proper English colony. I have, of course, told officials at Van Diemen's that it is obvious that the men are suffering a sort of mass hysteria.

There are no strange beasts.

Miss Geeves is not, herself, a monster.

It is all a creation of their minds. This new, strange land we find ourselves in is playing tricks upon their sanity.

I hope, in time, the men will forget they ever imagined the forest to be full of monsters. I hope that *they will soon call off their search and leave the wild forests for good.*

And I hope also, whatever the actual circumstances of Tessa's escape, that she now finds herself in a happy place.

Regards,

Isaac Livingston

'I saw them,' I said, as you put the book down on your lap.

'What do you mean, Tess?' you asked, your voice quiet and thin as tissue.

'I saw the creatures,' I repeated. 'Thomas Walter was not mad. I saw them too, and I have a feeling – a really strong feeling – that they have something to do with Cat disappearing.'

I only knew this to be true as I said it.

I had a flash, even as my mouth was opening, of a girl, tall and freckled just like you, running through the bushland, her face white and twisted with fear. I heard her heavy shoes crunching through the leaves and twigs. I heard her laboured breathing. And then I heard more footsteps, racing behind her, gaining on her more and more with every step. Almost reaching her, almost catching her . . .

And then the memory faded.

'Do you remember, Tess?' you asked. 'Do you remember Cat?'

'I think so,' I said.

You nodded slowly. 'And you say you've seen these . . . oh, Tess, look, I'm trying hard to stay calm but what you're telling me is . . . What *are* you telling me, exactly?'

'I think that Tessa Geeves – I don't know how to explain this, Connolly, but I *know* Tessa Geeves is me. When I woke up after my accident, I knew my name was Tessa. I didn't know how, but I *knew*. Now, in the same way, I know my name is Tessa *Geeves*, and that the girl in this book is me. I know it seems impossible, but –'

'It *is* impossible,' you interrupted. 'But you really do believe it, don't you?'

'I do. I also believe these creatures are real. Because I've seen them. And I've seen Cat.'

'Do you remember . . . did she seem safe?' you asked, and I saw veins begin to press hard against the thin skin on your temples.

I remembered again: the running, the fear.

I shook my head. 'No, Connolly. I'm sorry. I don't think she was safe.'

Tears sprang up in your eyes. 'Do you think – with your memories – we can find her?'

'I can try,' I said and then, thinking of Rhiannah and her bushwalks, 'I think I know where to start.'

Your eyes drifted to the clock on Rhiannah's bedside table. 'Oh, no,' you whispered. You turned to me. 'I have to go now,' you said, getting up unsteadily. 'I have to get back to the office. Vinnie is, well, you know what he's like, but he's in an especially bad mood at the moment. I don't think he's sleeping and so everything I do seems to be wrong. I can't be late back. But you'll call me, won't you, Tess? You'll let me know if you remember anything more about Cat. Anything at all.'

'I'll call you,' I said. I stood up too, and wrapped my arms around you. 'I'm going to figure this out,' I said.

'Thank you,' you replied, kissing me on the cheek.

'Thank you,' I whispered. 'For believing me.'

'I trust you, Tess,' you said. 'So I believe you, even though it's *really* hard.'

As you walked out of my bedroom door, you turned around and asked me one last thing, 'Tess, will you call yourself Tessa Geeves now?'

I shook my head. 'No, Connolly,' I replied. 'I want to stay being Tessa Connolly, if that's okay with you.'

You smiled. 'I'm so glad.'

You hugged me once more, and then you walked away, leaving me alone and wondering what to do next. Something was wrong with me. Something magical.

Something terrible. I had been a girl in 1851, and I was a girl now. And I had stripes.

I thought of Rhiannah and Harriet and Sara and what I had seen. I *knew* now they had jumped that wall. I sensed now that something big and wondrous was happening and it involved all of us. But my instincts told me that Rhiannah and Harriet and Sara were a different kind of being from what I was. They *didn't* have stripes like mine, and their scent was . . . wrong. Bad. Were they the enemy?

Where were they going on those bushwalks? Did it have something to do with Cat? Had *they* been involved in what happened to her? Even though Rhiannah was her friend? Had Rhiannah betrayed her?

I couldn't think about it. The idea filled me with a terror so huge that my entire body seemed crammed with it, pushing all other thoughts and feelings aside.

But I *needed* to think. I needed to remember. I needed to decide what to do next.

And I needed help.

I couldn't go to Rhiannah or Harriet or Sara.

I needed to go to the one person here at Cascade Falls that you said I could trust; the one person you said would look out for me; the person who had been your friend and confidante for so many years.

I needed to go to Ms Hindmarsh.

CHAPTER
twenty-five

I ARRIVED OUTSIDE MS HINDMARSH'S office with my head buzzing and swarming with words and sentences and ways to make her believe me; ways to make her *help* me. I held a curled hand up, ready to knock, when the door was wrenched open, and Mr Beagle launched himself out so quickly he nearly collided with my fist.

When he saw me, he jerked backwards and uttered a little yelp, his hand flying to his chest. I couldn't help smiling. Mr Beagle had seemed quite fierce, that first day when I met him on the school steps and he gave Laurel and Erin a dressing down for their naughty behaviour. Now, I liked him. He was still a bit grumpy – he always seemed like he hadn't had enough sleep – but he was a good teacher. He was smart and interesting, and passionate about history, and we got along very well. He did make a funny noise when he was startled, though.

'Ah! Tessa! You frightened me!' he said, smiling and looking nervously past me down the hallway.

'Sorry, Mr Beagle,' I said. 'I just came to see Ms Hindmarsh.'

'She's not here,' he said quickly. I heard his heart accelerate. I noticed tiny pearls of sweat on his forehead.

I noticed also that the grey circles beneath his eyes – the ones that seemed almost permanently stamped on his biscuit-coloured skin – were even more pronounced today. He looked as though he hadn't slept for a year.

'Oh, okay,' I replied. I was about to turn around and walk away, when something struck me. 'If she's not here, then what are you doing in her office?' I asked, feeling a rush of boldness. And suspicion. Maybe it was his anxious, guilty face, or the loyalty I felt to Ms Hindmarsh for being your friend, but I suddenly felt something was not quite right here.

'Well, I really don't think that's any of your concern, do you, Tessa?' he said, and I noticed for the first time that he held a book in his hand. I just made out the words 'Van Diemen Industries' on its spine before he tucked it hastily under his arm.

'Sorry, Mr Beagle,' I replied, because it seemed like the only thing I *could* say without getting into trouble.

I couldn't afford to get into trouble and end up in detention. I had too much to do.

Mr Beagle sighed. 'That's okay, Tessa,' he said. 'I'm sorry for snapping. I'm just tired, I suppose. Ms Hindmarsh had to go out unexpectedly to visit Mr Lord and she asked me to get some files for her. That's all.'

I didn't even bother to ask where the files were. He had none in his hand when he left the office – just the book. He was lying.

'Ms Hindmarsh will be back this evening,' Mr Beagle continued. 'Don't forget it's the full moon tonight. Mrs Bush is very keen that you all get a chance to observe it through our new telescope.'

I nodded, ignoring the way my scars began to throb every time the full moon was mentioned. 'I'll be there,' I said, returning his lie.

Of course, I wouldn't be there. If the whole school was in one spot, observing the moon, there seemed no better time for me to escape and begin my investigations. No better time for me to go on a bushwalk.

'Glad to hear it, Miss Connolly,' he said. 'I'm glad to hear you're not foolish and rebellious. The world out there is scary, Tessa. It's best to be sensible, if you're a young girl. Now, if you'll excuse me . . .'

And with that, Mr Beagle was gone.

I didn't have time to linger, though my meeting with

Mr Beagle had given me many more things to think about, and an intensified sense of unease. I could reflect about it later. Ms Hindmarsh was not in her office, and so my plans had changed.

Rhiannah had gone for her bushwalk hours earlier. And I wanted to catch up.

CHAPTER

twenty-six

It DIDN'T take as LONG as I thought it would to catch up with Rhiannah.

As I walked towards room 36, I heard raised voices. I crept closer and saw that the door to our bedroom was not properly shut. I crouched down and listened. For a moment the voices were silent, and I worried that I had been caught. But then they spoke again.

It was Rhiannah, and she was with Perrin. I could tell from the scent. I was distracted, briefly, by the memory of his face; the feeling of his hand in mine . . . but then I heard the tone of Rhiannah's voice, and it brought my thoughts sharply back into focus. Her voice wasn't jovial and joking, or kind and friendly. It was harsh and angry and, when I heard what the voice was talking *about*, it became terrifying. 'She has the stripes. If what the book says is true – if she is immortal – then that can only mean one thing. She's a Thyla. She's a Thyla who has been *sleeping in my bedroom* for the past week. Do you know how that makes me feel?'

She was talking about me. Rhiannah was talking about me. And she called me *Thyla*.

'And I believed her! Seriously, can you even believe how dumb I was? I bought her whole act of being human, of being a *friend*. I thought she'd lost her memory in the accident. Geez, Perrin, I thought she needed protecting! I thought: here was this new girl, this innocent human, just like Cat was. And, you know, Charlotte didn't like Cat either. She made her life hell. I couldn't let that happen again. Can you believe it? I should have killed her in her sleep!'

My breath caught in my throat. Did Rhiannah just say what I thought she said? That she should have *killed* me? A cold sweat began to prickle on my forehead.

'Rin, I know you don't mean that,' said Perrin. 'She's your friend.'

'She's a *Thyla*!' Rhiannah exclaimed. 'You know, the race that's been trying to wipe us out for millennia? Remember them?'

'If she'd been human, would that have been any better?' Perrin asked, his voice calm. 'Humans don't have the best track record with their treatment of our kind. Humans have sided with the Diemens in the past, and helped them become stronger. And you know, the Diemens are pretty damn strong now, Rhiannah. If what Rha says is to be believed, we may just *need* the Thylas on our side.'

'You really believe that?' asked Rhiannah, laughing bitterly.

'I believe what Rha says,' Perrin said, firmly. 'I believe there is something in this treaty idea.'

'You always believe what Rha says,' Rhiannah spat, and I pictured her rolling her eyes and crossing her arms. 'You worship him. It's pathetic.'

'What he says makes sense!' Perrin exclaimed, his voice getting louder. There was a pause, and when he continued his voice was soft again; measured. 'You're just scared. We're all scared. But we don't need to be scared of Tessa. Trust me on that, Rin.'

Rhiannah's voice was soft now, too. 'I know. I never would have given her the book otherwise. It just kind of threw me for six, you know? I never expected to bump into a Thyla *inside* Cascade Falls.'

'And I'm sure she never expected she'd be rooming with a Sarco either.'

Rhiannah sighed. 'Perrin, she barely knows about *Thylas*, let alone Sarcos. I think she's lost her memory. She keeps saying she doesn't know if she's done things before or eaten things before or whatever. Plus, she doesn't have a cuff, so she *can't* know who she is. No Sarco or Thyla in their right mind would go around among humans without a cuff, especially approaching a full moon. We may be able to switch in and out of this at will at other times of the month, but at a full moon? No, she really *must* have lost her memory. Oh, geez! Poor Tessa! I don't know why I said that before. I was just angry. And hurt. And . . . and scared.'

'If she's lost her memory, then we don't need to be scared of her. We need to look out for her. It's not just *approaching* a full moon, Rhiannah. It's a full moon *tonight*.'

'I know. I don't know what to do about that.'

'We do the only thing we can do. We go to the forest. We protect ourselves the best we can. And we wait to see what happens.'

'But what about Tessa?' Rhiannah's voice was anxious now, and small. She sounded like a scared child.

'I don't know. I really don't. I want to protect her, but it's not like *we* can be inside Cascade Falls when it's a full moon. It's too risky. And we can't take her with us either. Can you imagine taking a Thyla into Wellington Park with us on a full moon? One who doesn't know or has *forgotten* how to control her powers? One without a cuff to *help* her? It would be a catastrophe. I'm just going to have to ask you to suggest she stays in your room tonight. Will you do that? For me?'

'But what if someone finds her?' said Rhiannah. 'One of the humans?'

'If a human finds her on a full moon, pity that person, not Tessa.'

'We must have fought against her,' Rhiannah said, her voice sounding as though she was concentrating hard; straining to remember. 'That's the hardest thing. She would have been on the other side so many times, when I only knew her as a Thyla, not as a human, so I never recognised her. I keep telling myself I'm stupid, that I should have known.'

'You're not stupid, Rin. You couldn't have known. You never expected to find yourself sleeping with the enemy.'

'Very funny,' Rhiannah growled. 'And anyway, I thought you said she wasn't the enemy. I thought you said we should trust her. Why exactly do you think that, anyway? Is there something you're not telling me?'

'Don't worry, Rin. There's nothing you need to know,' Perrin said, firmly. 'Look, I gotta go, sis. Gotta get back to school. I'll catch you soon, okay?'

'Okay,' Rhiannah said, softly. 'You would tell me, though, wouldn't you? If there *was* something I needed to know?'

'There's not,' said Perrin, quickly. 'I'll see you soon.'

I heard Perrin's heavy boots clomping towards the door. Although I wanted to stay; although I was *desperate* to hear more, I did the only thing I could do.

I ran, with the lightest of feet, down the hallway and away.

CHapter
twenty-seven

THE GROUNDS WERE NOW filled WITH GIRLS. SCHOOL had finished, and everyone was walking towards their lockers or to the dormitories. They were gossiping and laughing. It was as if I'd stepped into a parallel existence – one where everything I had heard and everything I had discovered did not exist.

A world where everything was normal.

But even here I was still a freak. I *still* stood out.

Even without my scars or being . . . whatever it was I was, I stood out for running. I stood out for my casual clothes and tufty, unkempt hair. I stood out for the wild, anxious look on my face. Soon, everyone was staring at me.

And then, the whispers started.

'Look at her. She's *so* weird.'

That was Inga. I saw her rolling her pale blue eyes.

Then, there was another whisper. 'She looks like she's homeless.'

I saw Jenna shaking her strawberry blonde hair and fixing me with a sneer of disgust.

Then finally I heard Charlotte pretending to whisper, 'I don't know why she was ever let into Cascade Falls in the first place. Daddy is too kind for his own good. She's so wild. She's insane. The sooner she leaves here, the better. We don't have room for people like that. She's a beast.'

My heart seemed to stop as a memory burst abruptly into my head. I was hiding outside an office door, clasping a basket of clean washing. I was eavesdropping! There was a male voice, quiet and sounding as though the owner was quite upper crust. He was saying, *'We must eradicate these beasts. We must eradicate them if we are ever to fully control this colony.'*

And then another voice. *'But, sir. The men say they are human.'*

'They are not human, Hopkins. They are beasts. Vermin. Freaks of nature. They are an unruly, disruptive influence. Surely as a gentleman yourself you understand that. Surely as a gentleman you will be on our side.'

'But they were here before us,' another, familiar, voice interjected. *'Excuse my impertinence but, if you dislike them so, why do you stay here?'*

'*Who is this man, Hopkins?*' the first man growled.

'*His name is Livingston,*' said Hopkins. '*He is a guard here at the factory.*'

'*Some minor prison guard?*' the first man sneered. '*Why did you let him in here, Hopkins? Be off with you, man.*'

I heard footsteps as the third man retreated – though not completely. I didn't hear a door shut. He was hiding. Listening. Like I was. The first man proceeded, his voice quiet and menacing.

'*Hopkins, you know that every day Victoria remains Queen is another day that our power is diminished. Soon, we will have no power at all in our motherland. The convicts are being shipped abroad at an alarming rate. In England our game is slowly disappearing. And where the game goes, so must we! And, who knows, perhaps on the other side of the world, our kind will thrive once more. This place is our refuge. It is not the* best *choice, that much is certain, but it is our only choice. Our only option if we are to survive.*'

'*And the beasts? They prevent your survival?*'

'*They have been intercepting our sport; stealing our game. Transforming it into their own kind. It is a horror, what they do. What we do is . . . a kindness. You see that, don't you, Hopkins? We deal with the convict women much more humanely than they would be treated in the hands of the beasts.*'

'You have our support, sir. You know that. We are on your side.'

'Your loyalty will be rewarded, Hopkins. Just be sure you keep your side of the bargain.'

'We will provide you with women, sir. As many as you need. Don't worry, they won't be missed.'

'I see now it was a grand idea appointing you as warden of this prison, Hopkins. You have done us proud. And for that, we will grant you the highest gift we can bestow.'

'What is that?'

'Immortality.'

I heard a door click quietly shut. The prison guard had left the room. I needed to run. I needed to hide. If the guard found out I had been eavesdropping . . . but then, he had been eavesdropping too, hadn't he?

Still, I hid, curled up like a ball. I heard him run past. He was muttering to himself. 'They've gone mad,' he said. 'They've all gone mad.'

A darkness fell on my memory, and I was back in reality. I felt my body shaking. I didn't know what to do. I was surrounded by so many girls, all staring, all pointing, all whispering. I wanted to just sink through the ground and disappear.

Then there was another voice in my ear. A kinder one, saying, 'Come with me, Tessa.'

I turned around to see Ms Hindmarsh behind me, her arm outstretched. I had sought her and now she had found me.

I took her hand, pushing back the tears that threatened to break free from my eyes.

'I am Tessa. I am strong. I do not cry,' I whispered to myself.

I let Ms Hindmarsh lead me away to safety.

CHAPTER
twenty-eight

Laurel and Erin were sitting outside Ms Hindmarsh's office. I was grateful for their kind, accepting faces. They were not staring at me as though I was a monster, like the others had been.

'Would you mind waiting here please, Tessa?' asked Ms Hindmarsh, indicating towards the empty seat beside Laurel. 'I won't be long.'

I nodded and sat down.

As Ms Hindmarsh's door clicked shut, Laurel turned to me and asked, 'So, what are you in for?'

'What do you mean?' I asked.

'Don't mind her,' said Erin, twiddling a strand of her crackly black hair between her thumb and forefinger. 'She's in a stupid mood. That's why *we're* here.'

She shot Laurel a look that was dagger sharp.

'It completely was not my fault!' Laurel exclaimed, pouting.

'Oh yeah, somebody *made* you scratch "Mr Beagle is a very bad dog" into your desk with a compass,' said Erin, shaking her head.

She was trying to look serious, but her dimpled cheek let slip her true feelings.

'Nobody made you *laugh* when you saw it!' Laurel retorted, and the two of them collapsed into silly, helpless giggles.

I wanted to laugh too, but it wouldn't come. Looking at them giggling, I felt as though I was made of stone – like I was separated from their world, from happiness, by what I had learned and what it all might mean.

'You okay?' asked Erin, wiping tears from her eyes. 'You look a bit pale. Look, um, I heard something. Just gossip and, I mean, tell me if this is wrong, but I heard you had an accident before you came here? You were in hospital? Are you okay now?'

I nodded. 'I'm okay.'

Because, really, what else could I say? *No, I'm not okay. I actually think I might be an immortal monster, and my roommate is an immortal monster, too, and she wants to kill me in my sleep.*

No. Laurel and Erin were more kind and welcoming than anybody else at Cascade Falls had been, but I thought – to borrow a phrase Vinnie often used when he got grumpy with you – that might be 'pushing it'.

'Really? Well, if you ever need anyone, we're here. It's just . . .' Erin looked at Laurel, and Laurel shrugged, and nodded, as if to say 'go on'.

Erin looked back at me, her eyebrows scrunched together like two dark caterpillars kissing in the middle of her forehead. 'Okay, it's just that Laurel and I know it can be tough here. If you're an "untouchable". Princess Charlotte and those other cows think they own the place and, well, they kind of do. Mr Lord pretty much pays for everything, and the rest of their fathers are all big benefactors too. All of those girls' dads are Van Diemen Industries head honchos. Ours aren't. Our dads are just VDI labourers, and we only got in because of our scholarships. So we're never going to be good enough for those posh bitches . . .'

As if Erin's words had conjured them, Charlotte and Inga turned into the hallway, shooting us sharpened steel glares. As they strutted by, Inga said – without bothering to lower her voice – 'When are they going to kick those girls out of our school? It would be a much better place without them.'

'Daddy has always been a champion of the lower

classes,' Charlotte replied. 'I've always said his kindness is his biggest flaw.'

'Oi! I heard that!' said Erin, her lip curling.

'I know,' Charlotte replied primly as they walked away.

Laurel and Erin slowly raised the backs of their hands at the retreating figures of Charlotte and Inga and then folded down three fingers, leaving only the middle one standing. I giggled, despite myself. I could not remember *how* I knew the gesture was dreadfully rude. But I did. And those girls deserved it.

'Stupid cow,' Erin snarled, just as Ms Hindmarsh came out of her office.

'Laurel, Erin, I thought I told you both to stay silent out here,' she said, and I noticed a tenseness in her voice that I hadn't heard before; one that certainly had not been present the first time I'd encountered Laurel and Erin. Back then, it seemed as though their naughtiness amused her, and it was Mr Beagle doing all the grumping. Now, she seemed just as grouchy as he was.

She sighed and rubbed her temples. 'Come on, girls. We really need to get on top of this behaviour, don't we? Can I trust you two to be good out here while I have a quick chat to Tessa?'

Laurel and Erin both nodded, but I saw Erin's dimple fighting to press itself into her cheek again. I had a feeling 'good' wasn't a concept Laurel or Erin understood very well – or they *chose* not to. I wished I could spend more time with them. I would, but not now. Now, I needed to see Ms Hindmarsh. I leapt from my seat and was almost in the door before Ms Hindmarsh had a chance to invite me.

'Tessa, won't you come in?' she said, too late. She followed me inside, closing the door behind her, and walked over to her desk. She sat down stiffly.

'Take a seat, please.' Ms Hindmarsh indicated to the leather chair on the other side of the desk.

I sat, taking in my surroundings. I had been in here on my first day, but I'd been so overwhelmed I don't think I really noticed anything properly.

The office was quite plain compared with the opulent furnishings of the rest of the main building.

On the walls were two oil paintings that looked quite old. One was of a grand palace that looked familiar to me, as though I might have seen a painting or a photograph of it sometime before. Beneath the painting, in curlicued gold writing, was the word 'Buckingham'.

Buckingham Palace. I did know that building. It was where the Queen of England lived. *Victoria.*

The other painting showed a village street, with a church and clock tower. Beneath this painting were the words, 'Campbell Town, 1900.'

Campbell Town looks a pretty place, Connolly. Or, at least, it did one hundred years ago.

Aside from the paintings, the rest of Ms Hindmarsh's office was relatively sparse – just files and books and stationery items.

There was one other thing, though. One hint of personality.

It was a photograph on Ms Hindmarsh's desk. In it were two people. One was obviously Ms Hindmarsh, though she was much younger in the photo – perhaps twenty-five or -six. She had her arm around a tall man. He was handsome and dark-haired.

Something about him reminded me curiously of Perrin. It wasn't that they shared similar features in the way that brothers or cousins might. It was more a look in the man's eyes. A look of knowing something that others would never know.

My eyes jerked away from the photograph and up to Ms Hindmarsh. She was staring at me inquisitively, eyes narrowed. I could see the veins pushing against the skin of her temples, the tension in her jaw.

'What seems to be the problem, Tessa?' she asked tersely. It seemed as though she was a different person from the soft, jolly one I had met just a few days before. Even her bouncy curls had been subdued into a tight bun. Her lips were taut and she looked more gaunt and pinched. 'You seemed distressed in the hallway, which is why I felt I needed to bring you in here. To check you're okay. What's happened to upset you?'

Strangely, I found myself reluctant to confide in her. That strained voice and sober expression made me feel as though she wasn't on my side any more. I know it's queer, Connolly, and I know you asked me to trust her completely. But something in her eyes made me anxious.

'Tessa?' she said again. 'Come on. Something has clearly distressed you. I don't have much time, so I would appreciate it if you told me.'

I shook my head. 'No, Ms Hindmarsh. It's okay. I just wasn't feeling very well. I'm okay now.'

As I said it, a wave of pain passed over my scars. It was the worst one yet, and it made me jerk forward in my seat, my hands rushing involuntarily to my spine.

'You don't look okay, Tessa,' said Ms Hindmarsh, her voice now more gentle. She rose from her seat and began to move around her table towards me. Suddenly she paused, frozen on the spot. 'Is it your back?' she asked slowly, her voice barely more than a whisper. 'What's wrong with your back?' she repeated more commandingly when I didn't answer. There was a new heated fury in her eyes.

'It's nothing,' I replied. I was truly scared now.

'It doesn't look like nothing,' she said. 'Show me.'

'No, thank you,' I replied. 'Really, it's okay.'

'I said *show me*,' she snapped. She reached out towards me.

I leapt up from the chair and began to back away from her, my hands held up in front of me as though she was carrying a pistol.

'No, it's okay,' I said. 'Really. I think I'll just . . .'

And that's when I felt it. Something burning in my eyes, and a tightness in my mouth – a dreadful, pulsing, tightness.

My tongue, as if by some instinct, flicked towards my teeth and when it reached them, what it felt nearly made me vomit with shock and fear.

Sharp points.

Fangs.

As I looked about the room in panic I realised my eyes were keener than ever – every detail of the room was more clear and defined. And I could smell every single scent of Ms Hindmarsh's office separately and acutely, from the leather of the chair to the polish on the book-shelves to Ms Hindmarsh's own sharp citrus perfume.

I looked down at my hands. My fingernails had elongated and were now dark, their ends tapered and knife-like. I remembered, abruptly, what Rhiannah had said to me, on my first day here: *'Lovely hands . . .*

They look like they're used for great things. You can tell a lot about a person from their hands . . .'

I remembered, also, that they had done this before. That night at my window. That had been real.

I looked back up at Ms Hindmarsh, and was surprised to see that she was not displaying the same fear that I was feeling. After all, I was in front of her – a monster!

But she seemed calm. She seemed knowing. She nodded slowly and all the fire in her eyes was now gone, replaced with clinical coldness.

She began walking towards me.

cHapteR
twenty-NINe

tHe pHoNe's RINGING was LIke a scReam wItHIN my head, it was so loud and sudden and jarring.

Ms Hindmarsh stopped her slow progression and in that moment I reached out for the doorknob.

'Stop, Tessa,' Ms Hindmarsh said curtly. I turned to her and did something I never imagined I would do.

I bared my teeth. My *fangs*. Ms Hindmarsh's eyes widened.

'Don't come near me,' I said, calmly and slowly. 'You will regret it.'

Ms Hindmarsh nodded, her eyes wide. 'Yes,' she said. 'Yes, I think I would.'

I turned the doorknob just as Ms Hindmarsh picked up the phone. As I pulled the door open, I heard her say,

'Hello, Vinnie. I was hoping it would be you. Thank you for returning my call. Something has happened. I think we need to call him right away.'

Vinnie.

My heart thudded.

Ms Hindmarsh was talking to Vinnie about me. Vinnie knew about me.

They both did.

I slammed Ms Hindmarsh's office door and began to run.

'Tessa? You okay? What happened?' Laurel called after me.

I paused, but I didn't turn around. I couldn't let her see me like this.

'I'm okay,' I replied, my fangs feeling awkward in my mouth, making my words come out muffled and half-formed.

'Well, okey-dokey,' she said. 'But, you know, if you ever need us . . . Where are you going now?'

I didn't even have to think about it. 'I'm going with Rhiannah,' I replied. 'On the full moon walk.'

cHapteR
thirty

tHe aiR outsiDe was coot aND cRisp, aND it smeLLeD of eucalypts and mud and fresh water and old stone and decaying flesh.

My every sense was heightened. I smelled each scent individually. I heard each lizard darting through the grass, each currawong call, each wallaby bouncing over bracken. The coolness of the air enveloped me. It reminded me of the touch of some long-forgotten companion.

I walked upright still, but my legs felt different. Tauter and stronger and yet more flexible.

I felt *alive*.

I heard their footsteps – not so far away, just over the wall.

And it took me one sniff to confirm it: Rhiannah, Harriet, Sara.

They were close.

All that separated us was that high stone wall. The same high stone wall I had seen them so effortlessly overcoming in three swift, powerful leaps not so long ago.

I do not like walls. I want to jump them.

If they could do it, I could. I was every bit as powerful as they were. I could *feel* my power.

Another memory danced into my mind, pulling me close.

A man, naked and crouched before me, his face in shadows. The only features visible were the ones reflecting light. The eyes of amber and teeth like polished knives. I could see the stripes along his back and forehead. I could see his legs bending backwards.

'If you do this, Tessa, you will die. You know that.'

'But I will live again.'

'It will be different. You will not be yourself.'

He turned away from me, his head falling to his hands.

I did not let his warning make me fearful.

'I am not myself now,' I protested. *'If you turn me, that is when I will be myself. I will cease to be pathetic and powerless. I will take my revenge for what they did to my mother.'*

The man shook his head, looking up and away from me, towards the bush. 'I can't do this if I believe you will use the power for evil, Tessa. You know that. We talked about that.'

'They killed my mother!'

'And if I give you this power, you will be able to prevent that happening to others! That is a better gift than revenge.'

'I want to kill them. I want to kill Hopkins. I want to kill Chassebury.'

The man snorted, mocking me. 'If I do this, Chassebury will want to kill you. Your life will become dangerous!'

I rolled my eyes. 'Isaac, my life is already dangerous. All of us are in danger, as long as Lord is around.'

'But you know I have a plan to help you all. You don't need to do this, Tessa.'

'I want this. I want to help you.'

'You are willing to die for this cause?'

I nodded. 'I am willing to die.'

The memory dancer twirled away, and left me alone in the grounds of Cascade Falls.

'I am willing to die,' I murmured.

Then, like a punch to the stomach, another thought:

I am already dead.

That man said he needed to kill me for me to be like this. A monster.

Powerful.

Immortal.

I am those things now. I can feel it. I am one of *them*.

Who was he? The man with the amber eyes? I knew his voice.

That man killed me. I knew it. I knew it as surely as I had known those other things.

I am Tessa. I am strong. I do not cry.

And I am dead.

I looked at my reflection in the glinting metal of the school gates. My eyes were huge. Long sharp canines protruded over my bottom lip. My nose had flattened, the nostrils turned up. I felt unbearably hot so, without a thought of dignity or proper behaviour, I flung my blouse to the ground. Underneath, I was Thyla. Powerful, beautiful Thyla – striped and strong. I shivered – not from the cold, but from exhilaration. I was wondrous. I looked back at the wall.

'Well,' I whispered to myself, 'if I am dead, then what do I have to lose?'

I began to run.

CHAPTER
thirty-one

ONCE YOU HAVE FLOWN, THERE IS NOTHING ELSE.

I only flew for a moment – soaring high and mighty above the wall surrounding Cascade Falls – but it was extraordinary.

I conquered the wall.

I was free. And I was changed.

Inside the walls of Cascade Falls, I was Tessa. I was a human girl. I made friends. I wore a uniform. I ate waffles. I went to science class.

Outside of Cascade Falls, I was . . .

Well, I was still not entirely sure what I was. But perhaps human was the first thing I wasn't.

After all, humans cannot fly.

There was no time to think about the wonder of it all, though.

I could still hear their footsteps, cracking through the bracken. I could still hear their voices, low and rumbling and sodden with solemnity. I knew innately, through some new sense of time and space I seemed to possess along with my new, more powerful body, that they were close. And I knew now they were not on any ordinary bushwalk. I knew that their walks were part of all of this – Sarcos and Thyla and Chassebury and Cat.

And so I stalked them. I padded silently, growing more confident in my new gait. It was as though I had once known how to ride a horse, and then had not done so for many years, but was beginning again. My muscles knew how to do it. My brain just needed to catch up.

The forest was full and loud and brimming with the lives of the night creatures. Possums larked above me in the eucalypts. Quolls, pademelons and bettongs hopped and skittered through the brush. Above me, a masked owl whooshed through the leaves, hunting, and I could hear the terrified beating of tiny marsupial hearts.

'I can do that, too,' I whispered to the owl.

The pademelons had nothing to fear from *me*, though. There was only one group of beasts I was tracking. And I was closing in. I could hear their words clearly now.

'So you're sure the Diemens are on the hunt tonight?' came Rhiannah's voice.

My heart sped as I heard Perrin's voice come next. 'The Diemens are always on the hunt. That's why we're here. To stop them. And do you really think Lord donated that telescope out of the goodness of his heart? The more girls outside, the more vulnerable prey around, ripe for the picking.'

'I wonder what it's like in other places,' asked another voice. Sara. I knew she didn't need glasses in her new form. I wondered if she still wore her curls tied back with white ribbons. 'I mean, do you think there's anybody like us back in England? Is there anybody to stop them, or do they just run rampant?'

'I don't know,' said Perrin, and his voice sounded heavy and exhausted. 'I haven't *heard* of any other clans over there. Rha says that back in the convict days he heard about a tribe –'

'Perrin, we know this,' Rhiannah groaned. 'Honestly, sometimes you act like you're the only one who's been a Sarco all this time. Have you seen our hair? And our skin? We're starting to get the Sarco colouring. That means we've been doing this for a while. We're not clueless, you know. We know about the Vulpis.'

Vulpis.

The word snatched me from the present, from the bush, and dragged me back inside my head, where there was another memory waiting for me; another voice waiting to speak.

A man's voice, gruff and low.

'I do not know if we're the only ones, Tessa,' he said. 'There are rumours – some of the older Thylas talk of a master race back in England. They call them the Vulpis. "Victoria's foxes". They say that they are like us. They are an ancient race, as we are – older probably – and they, like we, now devote their lives to fighting the Diemens. To protecting the innocent.'

'Why are they called Victoria's foxes?' I asked.

'Queen Victoria, of course,' the man growled. 'She was the first monarch to attempt to combat the Diemens. Before Victoria, they ran rampant. They had free rein over the prisoners and street people. Nobody stopped them. Then Victoria started helping the poor and sending convicts to Tasmania, and the Diemens thought their days were numbered. That's why so many of them moved out here. Can you imagine? A whole island brimming with convicts. A captive colony of vulnerable, reviled wretches sent thousands of miles from their families. To the Diemens, it must have seemed that Tasmania was a table, laid out for a banquet feast. I have heard no estimates of how many Diemens

remain in the motherland, Tessa. I do not know if any of our brother Vulpis are keeping them controlled. Some say that the Vulpis have changed sides; that they are fighting for the Diemens now. Whatever the case, while Victoria reigns, the Diemens are weakened. When she dies, who knows?'

'Why did they not just kill Victoria?' I asked. 'They are powerful, are they not? And they do not seem to think murdering women is wrong. Would it not have been easier for them?'

'Perhaps. Perhaps Victoria is stronger than we imagine – stronger even than they. I have heard tell that they offered her immortality in return for turning a blind eye to their activities, and she refused. She is a formidable foe. A woman to be truly admired.'

'I will be formidable also,' I replied. 'I will be a foe to be reckoned with.'

'Do you regret your change?' asked the man, his voice even more rough now.

'No. Never. I am like Queen Victoria. I am like this for a reason. I know my duty. I will never surrender.'

Sara's voice pulled me away from the voices inside my head, and seemed, strangely, to echo them. 'Do you regret what you've become? Would you go back and refuse it? If you could? If it meant you got a normal life – a family maybe? I mean, we've nearly finished school and when we do . . . *years* after we've finished, we'll still look the same age. What will we do then? It scares me. We'll look sixteen forever, but we can't keep going to school and –'

'Sara, shush,' said Harriet. 'Now isn't the time for worrying about that stuff.'

'When *is* the time, then?' asked Sara. 'I get that I have maybe hundreds of years ahead of me, but sometimes I just want to know stuff *now.*'

I was very close to the Sarcos now. I walked more quietly, crouched low in the scrub. I hid behind trees. I knew how to stalk. I had done it before.

'Maybe none of us really have the answers, Sara,' said Perrin slowly, his voice gentle. 'Maybe even Rha doesn't have the answers. You know he's had to spend years in hiding to keep his secret. Maybe that's what we do – we just emerge into human society every once in a while . . .'

Perrin trailed off. From my hiding place, I saw his eyes swing around. I crouched lower. His nose twitched.

Oh, hell.

'What is it, Perrin?' asked Rhiannah. 'If you're worried about that Thyla smell, don't be. It's always like that around here.'

Perrin froze. He flicked his eyes away from my direction, back towards his sister. 'The Thyla smell lingers,' he said, simply, but I could hear the tremble of his voice. He knew I was there. Why wasn't he saying anything?

'Why do we have to do it at all?' asked Rhiannah, going back to their previous conversation. 'I mean, couldn't we just stay out here? In the wild?'

'Some Sarcos do. And . . . Thylas.' Again, his eyes flicked in my direction, and away. 'But we're all half-human. We're still connected to the human world. I know I would miss it.'

Perrin went silent for a moment, before continuing, 'To answer your question, Sara: No. I wouldn't go back. Not knowing what I do about the Diemens. I could probably try to fight them as a mortal, but they're just so powerful and the bastards are getting *more* powerful – as if I'd have a chance! We're meant to do this. Maybe it's what we were always meant to do. It's the one thing we have in common with the Thylas. We both have a responsibility and I wouldn't turn my back on that. But, you know, I'm only a baby by Sarco standards! Ask me when I'm Rha's age. Ask me in another hundred years.'

'Sometimes I wish the Sarcos hadn't come to our house that night,' Rhiannah said softly. 'I wish I could be normal again, and not have to spend my whole life out here, hunting those creeps. I wish we'd never moved down from Wynyard. Then this would never have happened. I wish I could go back to Mum and Dad; help them with their veggies and their market stall. I wish it was simple like that. Sometimes I even wish Mum and Dad had been there that night, so they could be Sarcos too. So we wouldn't be so alone. I wish we hadn't been changed. I wish we didn't have to do this. But then I think, if *we* don't do it, who will? I still don't think we should unite with the Thylas, though. They're our en–'

Rhiannah stopped and sniffed at the air, just like Perrin had done. But she didn't look in my direction. Instead, she looked to her left, and I saw her mouth the word, 'human'.

The Sarcos froze and talked no more.

I could still hear their hearts beating though. I could hear each one individually and it seemed as though I knew which heart belonged to which of my friends. If indeed they still were my friends.

The heart I heard most loudly – deep and full and resonant – I believed belonged to Perrin.

And I allowed myself, just for a moment, to enjoy the feeling of hearing his heart and mine. It was as though they were playing some rhythmic music together.

How was it possible, I wondered, to be dead and still have a heartbeat?

Especially since I had never felt more alive.

Perrin's heart quickened as the sound of feet crunching through the undergrowth echoed through the bush. It felt as though the whole world had stopped and was waiting, watching, to see who was making the noise.

Finally there was a voice. A new voice, but one I recognised. 'Hello? Is anybody there? It's just me, Ms Hindmarsh!'

My skin prickled.

I remembered the cold look in her eyes.

I remembered her slow, terrifying walk towards me, her arms outstretched. I remembered the hint of something sinister in her voice when she demanded to see my scars.

I remembered the phone call. *'Hello, Vinnie. I was hoping it would be you. Something has happened.'*

Ms Hindmarsh knew about me. And she wasn't scared.

And now she was *here*. It wasn't *right* that she was here.

Ms Hindmarsh wasn't to be trusted. I could smell it.

But I could also smell the terror of the Sarcos fading away. They weren't scared any more. They trusted Ms Hindmarsh.

'Rhiannah, Harriet, Sara? Is that you?' Ms Hindmarsh called out.

'It's us, Ms Hindmarsh!' Rhiannah called back. 'We're just finishing up our bushwalk. We'll be coming back soon!'

'I'm with them, Cynthia. Don't worry!' Perrin added.

Cynthia.

Perrin called Ms Hindmarsh by her first name. They must be friends.

Then I remembered the dark-haired man in Ms Hind-marsh's photo – the one who'd reminded me of Perrin. The hair, the pale skin, that knowing look in their eyes.

'Well, that's good, Perrin,' said Ms Hindmarsh as she walked into sight. 'You never know when one of your own might need protecting.'

'Cynthia.' Perrin's voice became tender, and I saw him lope over to Ms Hindmarsh, while the other Sarcos shrank back against the trees. Ms Hindmarsh only had human eyes. She couldn't see them. As he left the others, I heard him hiss something in some strange, foreign language of growls and squeals. Sarco language. I did not understand it, but I looked quickly to Rhiannah and the others and I saw that they were hastily pulling bangles from their backpacks and pushing them onto their wrists.

And that was when I knew.

That's what Perrin had been talking about when he said I had no 'cuff' to control my powers. The bangles were how they controlled it.

I didn't have a bangle. I had no control.

'Why are you out here tonight, Perrin?' asked Ms Hindmarsh. 'I mean, really? You told me you were just patrolling. But there are so many of you. You're not hunting are you? For humans to . . . turn.'

'No, of course not,' Perrin said. 'Why would you say that, Cynthia? You know we don't do that. You've told us before that you know what happened with Raphael was just an accident.'

'What happened to Raphael was not just an *accident*,' Ms Hindmarsh snapped. 'You beasts did it. You did it on purpose. Forget it. You're not on my side. You never were. I believed you could help me, for a while . . . but now I have someone else. Someone much more powerful than you are. Someone who is going to help me get Raphael back. *Properly back.* The way he used to be.'

Vinnie. Ms Hindmarsh must be talking about Vinnie.

'What do you mean?' asked Perrin.

'I have friends in high places now,' said Ms Hindmarsh, a bitter laugh behind the words.

'No,' said Perrin, his voice hard now. 'No, Cynthia. You haven't . . .'

'I have powerful friends who are going to get Raphael back. And you are going to help us.'

'Cynthia, think about this. You know how evil –'

Perrin was moving towards Ms Hindmarsh, his hands held palm-up. He looked over her shoulder at the other Sarcos hidden in the bush. His expression was unreadable.

'No, Perrin,' she said, holding her hands up in front of her. 'They are not evil. They want to help. They've helped me enormously with the school and they've helped the girls – most of them. The ones who deserved it. The ones who didn't, well . . . they got what they *did* deserve,

I suppose. Small sacrifices. For a greater good. They are not evil. They are *benevolent*. It's you *beasts* who are evil.'

'But I thought . . . you knew we wanted to help you find Raphael. We want it as much as you do.'

Ms Hindmarsh nodded. 'Well, that would suggest that I believe that Raphael is missing. I don't. I know where he is, just as I know what became of those girls that were taken from my school. Ha! Don't look at me like that, Perrin. Like I've sold my soul to the devil.' Ms Hindmarsh paused as if waiting for laughter after her joke. When there was none, she continued. 'Sometimes, sacrifices must be made in the course of higher purpose. Raphael is my purpose. I will have him back, just as soon as Lord is finished. It's better this way. Do you have any idea how difficult it was for me, pretending he was missing, when really he was with you *brutes*? How it felt knowing he wanted the wildness; that he wanted to be away from me? Perrin, I've known all along where Raphael is. I only pretended I didn't. Lord thought that was best. He needed you to trust me. Ted Lord has been *very* helpful to me, Perrin. And he only wanted one small thing in exchange.'

'And what was that?' asked Perrin.

'You.'

Ms Hindmarsh whirled around and called out to the darkness around her, 'They're here! Come and get them! They're here!'

cHapteR
thirty-two

THE NEXT few moments were some of the most terrifying of my life.

After Ms Hindmarsh yelled out, the forest exploded in a flurry of yelling, rushing figures, breaking branches and screaming.

Men burst from the trees behind Ms Hindmarsh.

I call them 'men', but it was obvious immediately that they were not ordinary men. Their faces were pale and almost metallic-looking, with a sheen that glimmered in the moonlight. When they opened their mouths, instead of teeth, they had fangs, as we did.

But their fangs were as silver as polished knives. In their hands they carried daggers, long swords, axes. And guns.

'No!' Rhiannah cried. 'Ms Hindmarsh! No!'

'They're here! Lord, they're here!' Ms Hindmarsh repeated, calling the men forward.

And they came. So quickly, they came. There must have been at least fifty of them, moving through the bush in a way that was not walking, nor floating, but something in between. At their head was a man in his forties, dressed in a suit of darkest indigo blue. His hair was pale as frost, his eyes like a frozen river. He looked exactly like Charlotte Lord.

And he looked like Sir Edward Chassebury.

'Come, men!' he called, and his voice was like the quiet loading of a hunter's gun. And I knew as soon as he spoke that he did not simply *look* like Chassebury. He *was* Chassebury.

The man who killed my mother.

My blood flowed hot. Claws scraped my palms as I made my hands into fists.

'Perrin?' Rhiannah cried, her voice strangled and trembling. 'Perrin, there's so many of them. What do I do?'

'Take your cuff off,' Perrin hissed. 'Then just do what comes naturally.'

Four copper bangles fell to the ground.

And though I should have gasped at what I saw in front of me – my roommate and classmates becoming animal – it was when they found their true forms that I felt I knew them best.

The Sarcos stripped their blouses and shirts, leaving their torsos naked.

I watched, holding my breath. Perrin in his Sarco form was very different from Perrin in his human form. He seemed even bigger and stronger. His broad chest was now part white, part black, and its muscles were taut and . . . *delicious.*

I forced myself to look away from him. I looked instead at the others.

Their skin was now black, mottled with white. Their noses were longer – almost like snouts – and their ears were higher and larger. Their eyes were narrower and further forward. Their hands grew sharp claws. Their legs bent back inside their trousers. They were Sarco.

I found them awesome and terrifying all at once.

And then it began.

Perrin's roar was like a war cry. The four Sarcos leapt forward, covering the space between them and Lord's men in a fraction of a second and enveloping them in a haze of claws, teeth and fists. Guns fell to the ground as the men struggled against the brutish power of the beasts. I could barely make sense of what I was seeing. Though my Thyla senses made it easier to distinguish body from body, the frenzied rhythms of the fight still blurred the images in my head. There were no gunshots, but I could hear the sickening raking of sword against flesh. I could hear screams of pain. I could see bodies dropping to the ground, then struggling to stand again and continue fighting. It was difficult to see who was winning. It seemed, for now, that the two sides were evenly matched. But for how long?

My heart thudding, I squinted and craned, certain that one body at least had not moved since falling.

It was certainly a Sarco. And female.

One of my friends was dead.

The Sarcos were fighting well, and I couldn't just watch them struggle and fall. I needed to help.

But I didn't know if I had ever fought before. I could not remember.

'For pity's sake!' I growled at myself. 'Just *remember*!'

And then it came back. Shadows into light. Memories of fighting. Of *me* fighting. Of me punching and biting. Biting men. Biting humans. Of me roaring, '*Stay away from her! Leave her alone! She's not yours to take!*'

Of the cold, metallic voice of Lord saying, 'They're all mine. When will you vermin understand that? They are worth nothing to anyone except to me. They are all mine!'

And then flying fists, gouging claws: his hands; my claws.

Edward 'Ted' Lord. Sir Edward Chassebury.
I had fought Lord Chassebury before.
I could do it again.
I poised to pounce.

CHapteR

tHIRty-tHRee

tHe aRm tHat wRappeD aRouND my tHRoat was LIke a vice – heavy, painful, unyielding.

I opened my mouth to scream, but before I could a hand pressed hard against it. I struggled and writhed and jabbed at my attacker with my newly powerful limbs, but I could not shake them. They were stronger than I was.

They must be immortal, too, I thought.

I felt their breath against my ear, and then they were speaking.

And I knew this voice too.

'Ssshhh, Tessa. It's okay. It's only me. I need you to turn around very slowly. Don't make a sound. Please. Trust me.'

How could I trust him? After what I had heard?

'*Hello, Vinnie. I was hoping it would be you . . .*'

How could I trust him when I knew he was in league with her? With the one who had just invited a group of monsters to slaughter my friends?

It was as though he could read my thoughts. 'You think I'm one of them, don't you?' he whispered. 'Nothing could be further from the truth. Sometimes, Tessa, to destroy the thing you hate you must become it.'

Vinnie's breath was hot in my ear. I struggled less as I listened, wondering what his story really was; wondering if I should believe it. 'I left my home for a century,' he continued. 'I have had to work, as Vinnie, for many years to gain their trust and, without it, I would not have known about tonight's attack. Cynthia and Lord both think I am on their side. I am not. I will explain more, but turn around and you will see I am telling the truth. Can I trust you to do it silently?'

I nodded, my chin pressing into the palm of his hand. He let go and I turned around.

And it was all I could do not to fall to my knees.

In front of me was Vinnie. But not the same Vinnie I remembered from the hospital and the police station. Not the Vinnie in the worn suits with a cardboard cup of coffee permanently attached to his hand, and the bags upon bags beneath his eyes. Not the one who grunted and grouched and slouched about as if the weight of mountains pressed against his shoulders.

He was nothing like *that* Vinnie, and yet I knew it was him. I could hear it in his voice and smell it on him. He did not smell like strong cologne any more. He smelled like . . . like musk and sweat and blood. I recognised his scent.

This Vinnie had fire in his amber eyes – they flickered and sparkled. This Vinnie stood tall, his muscles tensed.

This Vinnie had stripes.

And claws.

He was a Thyla. His eyes were larger, rounder, and the iris nearly eclipsed the white. His nose was broader and flatter, and his nostrils turned forwards, like a dog's. His ears were bigger too, and pointed. His teeth had been replaced by fangs. His body seemed more lithe, and his muscles were harder and more defined. He wore trousers still, like the Sarcos did (thankfully – I think I may have fainted if he were wholly naked) and yet I could see his legs bent backwards. His torso was bare, and I could see stripes when he twisted away. He was still human in some ways and yet he was *other* as well. He was *Thyla*. Like me.

'You're . . .' I began.

'Since 1851,' he said, attempting a smile. 'Just like you. Isaac Livingston is my proper name.' He held out his broad, clawed hand, grabbed mine and shook it roughly. 'I don't think we have time for more niceties than that,' he whispered. He looked towards the clearing. 'The Sarcos are managing now, but they need to more than manage. I have reinforcements coming. As soon as they're here . . .'

I tried to shake the shock out of me. 'Isaac Livingston!'

The prison guard from the Female Factory. The man who wrote the report about me. The man I remembered in the room when the overseer was talking to Chassebury. That was *Vinnie*? And he was a *Thyla*?

I had so many questions.

He was right, though. We didn't have time. I just had one question I *needed* answered before I could truly trust him. I spoke quickly. 'How did you do it?' I asked. 'How did you hide what you are from Lord? If he knew you at the Factory, he must have wondered how you . . .'

Vinnie read my thoughts. 'Like I said, I disappeared. Fled to the bush. Became Thyla almost full-time and watched them. With you. You'll remember that, eventually. It was only a hundred years later, when I saw how they were becoming more ruthless in their actions, that I re-emerged. I dyed my hair to look older. I wore different clothes. Strong aftershave so he couldn't detect my Thyla scent. I was insignificant to Lord back in the day – a mere lowly prison guard. He didn't remember me.'

Isaac looked up, past my shoulder.

'Ah, Beagle,' he said.

Beagle?

I swung around. Mr Beagle (well, a Thyla who looked and smelled something like Mr Beagle) crept stealthily through the forest. Behind him were another ten Thylas.

'Isaac,' said Mr Beagle, nodding. It was definitely him. The voice was the same. 'Tessa.'

'Hi, Mr Beagle,' I said meekly. I had a million questions for him, but the most pressing one was, *Did you know? And if you* did *know, why didn't you tell me?*

But my questions would have to wait. I stayed silent and listened.

'Are we ready?' asked Vinnie. *Isaac.*

Mr Beagle nodded, and looked back over his shoulder at more Thylas, creeping out of the darkness. 'As we'll ever be,' he whispered.

'Then let's go,' said Isaac.

'Is she coming, too?' asked Beagle.

'Of course,' Isaac replied. 'She's done it a million times. A hundred and sixty years' worth.'

'But she's for–'

'She'll remember. We need her out there. You know she's a pro at this. She'll remember.'

Beagle nodded. And so, I was in.

Isaac nodded back at Beagle and then, a sharp claw held to his lip, he nodded over Beagle's shoulder at the other Thylas.

This was really happening. It was about to begin.

CHAPTER
thirty-four

WE HAD SURPRISE ON OUR SIDE, BUT THAT WASN'T AN
advantage for long.

For the first few moments after we burst into the
clearing where the battle was taking place, it seemed as
though we were on top. We knocked men to the ground
with our blows, stabbing at their chests with our claws,
biting at their necks with our sword-sharp teeth. They fell
like fish from a waterfall.

And I was in the middle of it. Isaac was right: I *did*
remember.

It wasn't easy. I was scared. I wondered if I had always
been scared of this: of fighting, of the Diemens. Because
they were horribly scary. And evil. You could see it in
their eyes; in the way they smiled as they killed. We did

not smile as we killed. We winced and grimaced. But we had to do it. To protect my friends.

We Thylas called out warnings and instructions to each other in yips and cough-like barks that only we could understand; sounds that I remembered more easily than I remembered many human words. The noises were instinctive. They were part of me. The Sarcos communicated in their own secret language that sounded like growls and screams.

I had Diemen blood on my tongue. It tasted like poison. I spat it to the ground and it sizzled.

Their blood was black.

As I fought, I added what I learned in battle to the list of things I knew.

I am Tessa. I am strong. I do not cry. I am dead. I am a killer.

And though I felt remorse for it – though the human inside me was ashamed of the pain I was causing – I was certain that I was doing the right thing.

It was instinct.

And it was memory.

I knew that Lord's men were evil.

I *remembered*.

Lord and his followers came to Tasmania because this is where the convicts were. The convict girls and women. Before they killed them, they inhaled the last breath of their victims. And once they had killed them, they ate their heart and bathed in their blood. This was their bloodsport. They were hunters. This was also how they became immortal, a sort of vampire, except, like us, they could be fatally wounded.

The Diemens targeted the convict women because they thought nobody would miss them.

But somebody *did* miss one of them.

I missed my mother.

And the Thylas, though many had no humans to miss any more, missed a time when everyone – human and shapeshifter – was free to roam the bushland as they wished and without fear. When everyone could truly be wild. They hated Lord's men for taking their freedom, and the freedom of the women they attacked.

I remembered them fighting beside me as though my battle was their own, and I fought as though theirs was mine.

And as I bit and punched and clawed, I remembered something else: *'There are not enough prisoner women now to sustain them. They have been forced to start hunting civilians.'*

The words repeated in my head in Isaac's voice, and a chill ran through me even as my body flamed and burned and battled.

I remembered it, Connolly. Finally I *saw* it. The most important memory of all.

A girl who looked like you. Running. Terrified. Another girl behind her. A girl with white hair. A girl closing in, calling out, 'Daddy! I've found her! I've found her for you!'

Me, leaping through the trees, misjudging my footing, falling behind.

They caught her. And it was my fault.

But I found her again, Connolly. I remember now. I found her again and we were friends. Cat and I were *friends*.

Holy hell. How did I forget that?

She was there the night I fell. It was a night-time patrol. Cat and I were paired up, searching the forest for signs of Diemens. She was trying out her new powers by jumping about on the rocky cliffs, deep ravines and crevasses all around her. I begged her to be careful.

I called out to her yet again, '*Cat, watch it!*'

'*I'm fine!*' she called back. '*You're watching me. I'll be fine. Why don't you come up here and play with me, Tess? It's fun!*'

'*We are meant to be patrolling!*' I protested. '*This is not the time for fun!*'

'*It's not dangerous up here, Tessa!*' she said. '*Look, follow me! I'll show you what I can do now!*'

I groaned inwardly, and made to follow, but then I heard it: footsteps pounding through the bush. At first I thought it was Cat coming back, but then I smelled them. *Diemens*.

'*Lord's going to be so pleased with us,*' one of them was saying. '*Got the solution here safely* and *a subject to test it on.*'

I crouched down. The Diemens were walking towards me, only a few metres away. They had another with them. Not a Diemen. A Sarco, by the smell. He was only half-turned, though. His legs were only slightly wrong-facing, pushing against the backs of his trousers. His hands didn't yet have their claws. They were bound and he had a hessian bag over his head.

'*Enough solution here to last us a while,*' one of the Diemens said. '*Good thing, too. I hear it's hard to make, and Lord had to pull some serious strings to get it shipped over from England. Greedy bastards wanted to keep it all for themselves.*'

The solution. I did not know what it was but I knew that if it was in the hands of Diemens – and if they had a captive Sarco to test it on – it could not be good. I had to get it from them. And save the Sarco.

The Diemens had moved farther away now, so I knew I would not be heard. But they were not too far away for me to catch them, if I ran at my top speed. I was good at running quietly. I would be upon them before they knew it.

I moved carefully along the high ledge. But I was not as careful as I should have been. I lost my footing and slid silently down the cliff. And that is all I remember.

I failed. But I would not fail again.

I clenched my fists and looked up at the battle in front of me, just as another Diemen launched himself at me.

I deflected his attack; pushed him away with all my newfound might. The man fell backwards, but he was smiling, a sickening, twisted smile full of silver teeth.

'This is only the beginning, Thyla,' he snarled as he sprang back to his feet.

'You seem awfully confident,' I replied, shifting my stance and steadying myself.

'Oh, I am,' he said, moving forwards. 'We have the solution now. It's only a matter of time before what we have been waiting for these many years is finally realised.'

I launched myself at him, fangs bared. But he was quicker than I. He grabbed my arm and pulled me close. 'Too many years of waiting,' he whispered. He pushed his dagger against my throat. 'We know what we're doing now. We know how to test it, how to perfect it. You just wait, you filthy –'

Then his eyes bulged and a trickle of black blood oozed from his charcoal lips.

His grip eased on my arm and he slumped to the ground. Standing behind him was Perrin.

'Don't you die, little girl,' he growled. His eyes seemed to pierce my skin and my breath became sharp and ragged.

'Hey, Tessa!' a voice called out to me above the wailing

and roaring and pounding of the fray. I tore my eyes away from Perrin.

Another man leapt at me and I stuck my claws deep in his neck. Rhiannah was beside me, her arm twisting the head of another of Lord's men.

'Hey, Rhiannah,' I cried.

'When this is over, we'll go and get waffles, okay?' she yelled.

'Definitely,' I yelled back, allowing myself a smile.

And that's when it happened. In that small moment of distraction, Rhiannah was taken.

Lord, his white hair glinting in the moonlight, swept down like a goshawk and clamped his arm around Rhiannah's throat so tightly that her scream turned to a moan.

Then he looked me right in the eyes.

And he smiled.

My blood turned to ice.

In a fraction of a second they were gone.

Then Lord's men – the ones who had survived – retreated too, without a word or a backwards glance. They had come to us in a flash, like lightning, and they were gone every bit as quickly.

And we were left – the ones of us who survived – stunned and panting. Once we could breathe again, the forest echoed with our cry.

'Rhiannah!'

CHAPTER
thirty-five

PERRIN TRIED TO CHASE THEM. HE TRIED TO GET HER back. But he returned to us alone, and with a face that looked as though it was made of marble. He shook his head. 'They disappeared,' he murmured. I felt as though my heart would explode.

'But shouldn't we even *try?*' I cried, pushing the sobs back down my throat. *I do not cry.*

Perrin shook his head. 'They will have set up sentries to trap us. If more of us go now, unprepared, we will all be killed. We need to make a plan. Rhiannah is in danger. We don't want to put her – or any of the rest of us – in *more* danger. Besides, we don't know where to go. We don't know where they hide; where their headquarters are.'

Isaac continued. 'Lord lets me in only as much as he needs to. I only see him on neutral territory. Perhaps if I allowed myself to be changed into a Diemen, he'd let me in more, but I have him convinced it's better that I stay "human". They need someone who doesn't need to feed the way they do – someone who doesn't need to hunt – to be their eyes and ears while they're doing so. This has its advantages – I don't need to transform into a blood-bathing psychopath – but it also means we don't know where their den is. In times like this, that would be useful –'

Perrin interrupted. 'You *will* promise me you won't go off after her, okay, little girl? I know you want to protect her, but I won't let you get . . .'

He trailed off. I felt anger flame deep in my belly.

'Little girl'. He always called me that. I hate how he calls me that.

I glared at him. Made my Angry Tessa face.

But even as anger bubbled and boiled within me, the pull towards him grew stronger. I wanted to go to him. I wanted to put my arms around him and say it would be better. I would make it better. It was only Isaac's presence that prevented me.

And the knowledge that I would have been lying. Rhiannah had been taken. I had no idea how to make that better.

None of us knew. What we did all know was that despite the hundred and sixty years of similar fights behind us, this time it was different. For one thing, there was Ms Hindmarsh. Through gaining her trust, Lord had infiltrated Cascade Falls. We wondered how many other people there were working for Lord, embedded in places he could use for his . . . *game.*

And Rhiannah had been taken. Alive. The other Sarcos didn't know why she had been taken. Not yet. But I did. I told Isaac what the Diemen had whispered to me, and I told him what I saw on the day of my accident.

'This is not good,' he murmured. 'It's starting.'

I didn't ask Isaac what 'it' was. I knew. 'It' was the Solution. 'It' was the thing we Thyla and Sarcos had feared for centuries. 'It' was the Diemens finally achieving enough power to truly balance ours.

I looked around me, to the other Thylas and Sarcos. To the others who would share this struggle.

The Thylas stood on one side of the clearing and the Sarcos on the other. The air between us was filled with tension and with unbearable pain.

On the forest floor were two of our own, slain. One Thyla. One Sarco. There were at least five of Lord's men as well, face down in the mud. They were beginning to sizzle and melt into blackness, but their defeat did not come close to compensating for our loss.

Mr Beagle was dead. I had seen him fall, and heard Isaac's tortured howl as he saw it too. They were friends.

Sara was dead too. I could see her curls, now matted down with blood and mud.

They still had white ribbons woven around them.

We mourned. And yet we did not mourn together. We were in two camps: Sarcos and Thylas. I remembered now that it had always been this way.

In the middle of them all, so perfect and peaceful she might have been dreaming, lay Ms Hindmarsh – your friend, Connolly. I'm sorry. I don't know how she died. I don't know who did it. I don't know if it was Thyla or Sarco, or even Diemen. But she's gone. If it was a Thyla who did it, you'll forgive us, won't you? You'll forgive me and Isaac? We had to do it, Connolly.

She made us do it.

I looked over at Perrin, who had moved away to stand with Harriet. She had her arm around him. I felt a stab of jealousy but I brushed it away. I didn't even *know* Perrin. There was no reason for me to feel this way and yet . . . I closed my eyes and I felt his lips on mine. I felt his strong arms around my waist. And it wasn't like a dream. It was like a memory. But that was ridiculous, wasn't it? I was just being silly. He was a stranger, and he was rude and ungentlemanly.

And he was a Sarco. And I was a Thyla.

I turned to Isaac. His face looked just as grim as Perrin's.

'Are we going to move them?' I asked. 'Are we going to bury them?'

'We don't move them, Tess. You really have forgotten everything, haven't you?'

'I'm remembering,' I said, defensively. 'Just . . . not this part. Yet.'

Isaac sighed. 'All right. You have to get it all back soon, though, okay? It's bloody annoying.' He broke off and looked over at the bodies. 'Look, Tess,' he said. 'It's already starting. That's why we leave them.'

I looked again at the bodies. My stomach churned as I saw parts of them had turned to dust. They were fading away.

'They rot and then become the soil we walk on,' Isaac continued. 'It happens much more quickly than it does with human corpses. They'll have joined the soil again in a matter of minutes. Their bodies won't be seen or found. The Diemen bodies will disappear, too, but they become blood that seeps into the soil. In this way, the humans they have murdered – whose blood they have fed upon – become part of nature and, I suppose in a way, alive again. It's natural for us, Tessa. Only humans bury their dead. And besides, they were dead already, technically.'

Dead already. As I was.

Isaac must have noticed the pained look on my face, because he shook his head and said, 'That came out wrong, Tess. Sorry. When I say they were dead – when we are bitten and we gain the ability to shapeshift, to change from human to Thyla or . . .' Isaac glanced over at the other pack across the clearing, and his voice became a growl again, just for a moment. 'Or *Sarcos*, our old lives die. Our heart stops beating and our lungs stop working but, with the next gust of wind, we breathe again and our heart starts to beat again, and we are *born* again. A new life. Even if some of us are never entirely free of our old lives.'

I knew without asking what Isaac meant. Even though he had a new life as a Thyla, he would never stop trying to defeat Lord. And even though I was changed, too, I would never forget my mother's death. I would continue to try and make it right.

'When this new life ends though, Tessa, we become soil, just like everything else. We're all equal in death.'

So that is how I died. I was bitten. I stopped breathing. My heart stopped beating. And this is how I will live. Thyla.

'Did you always know it was me? That I was Thyla?' I asked.

'Of course,' said Isaac. 'You have been by my side this whole time. For more than a century and a half.'

'Then why didn't you tell me?' I blurted. 'Why didn't you tell me who I was?'

Isaac looked at his feet. 'Because it was me who made you like this. I always felt guilty for it. I wanted you to have a chance to be normal again, even for just a little while.'

'*You* made me Thyla?' I whispered.

'After Lord killed your mum, I knew you'd be next. He had his sights on you. You'd known I was a Thyla for a while, of course, although you didn't know the name for it. You caught me one night. You sneaked out of bed, and you found me in the courtyard at the Female Factory, looking like this. You begged me to change you then, but I resisted. I thought that maybe if I just looked out for you, you'd be okay. You could stay human. You could lead a normal life, without all of *this*.'

'I'm glad you changed me,' I whispered. 'I wish you changed Mum too, so she could have survived. I wish she was still here. But I'm glad that *I* am here. This is who I'm meant to be. I may not remember it, but I feel it.'

'Yeah, well, it's not all hearts and flowers, as you can see,' Isaac said.

I followed his gaze to the third body in the clearing. The only human one. The only one who would be found.

'Funny the things people will do for love,' Isaac murmured.

'Her husband was a Sarco?' I said. 'Raphael?'

'*Is*, as far as we know,' said Isaac. 'Though nobody's seen him for a while. It may be that he was the Sarco you saw, in which case . . .' Isaac paused, his eyes looking faraway, a grimace twisting his mouth. My stomach lurched as I thought of what Raphael might be going through. And Rhiannah. Oh, hell.

'Cynthia knew that Raphael had been turned,' Isaac said finally. 'She hated it. She wanted her human husband back. One night, in a meeting with Lord – I was there – she confided in him that something had "changed" about Raphael. Of course, Lord knew exactly what she meant. Lord told her he could change Raphael back. He told her he had some new technology for turning shapeshifters back into humans.'

'The solution.'

'That's what they're calling it. I really don't know that much –'

Isaac was interrupted by a hand on his shoulder. As he turned, I saw a tall Thyla standing behind him, their face half-veiled in shadow.

The figure moved sideways and I saw that it was a female. Her markings were light and, on her snout, looked almost like freckles.

'Hi Tessa,' she said.

'Hi Cat,' I replied. My voice sounded calm but my heart was beating like a military drum. Cat Connolly was standing in front of me. She had survived.

Cat laughed, throwing her head back. 'I thought you said she'd forgotten me,' she said to Isaac. He shrugged.

'I only just remembered,' I admitted.

The girl walked towards me, and flung her arms around me.

'Tessa, ya doofus. I *knew* you wouldn't forget me. You're the one who saved my life! If it wasn't for you I'd be Blood Bather prey.' Cat leaned out, her face serious now. 'Look, I'm really sorry for leaving you that day on the mountain. If I hadn't run off, you might never have fallen. I didn't get far away before I realised you weren't with me. I started to come back, but then I heard the Diemens coming through the bush and I had to hide for a bit in a little cave. Once they'd gone, I went back to where I left you. When I saw you lying at the bottom of the cliff, my first thought was that they'd done something to you. But I knew they wouldn't have just left you there. Like that. They would have roughed you up a bit more. They can't help themselves – the bastards. You were pretty lucky the Diemens didn't hear you fall, or if they did, I guess they thought it was just a rock fall 'cos they didn't turn back. Anyway, I could see how bad your injuries were and I knew we couldn't fix you. We heal faster than humans, but even though you'd improve quickly, I didn't know if you'd *survive* long enough to get there. So I just put your cuff on and rang . . . well, Mum, as it turns out. But she didn't know it was me, thankfully. I decided at the last minute to put on this stupid accent. Lucky I did, hey? God, I feel really stupid thinking I did that now. I was still so new to this. I was still in the human mode of "when in danger, call the police". I'm smarter now.'

Cat – my *friend*, Cat – smiled again.

I wondered how she was able to smile when her friends had just been killed.

Perhaps it is just as Isaac said – death is normal. It is the way of things. Perhaps Cat knew this.

I could not smile back, though. I grieved. I ached for my lost friends.

And I also ached for you, Connolly. Cat was alive and you were still yearning for her and searching for her. And she was *thankful* you hadn't recognised her voice!

'Your mum thinks you're dead!' I cried. I couldn't keep the accusation, the *anger*, from my voice.

Cat's smile faded. 'I know,' she whispered. 'I hate that. I hate hurting her so much. But Isaac has been looking out for her, haven't you, Isaac? He got her to come to the city, and he's been taking care of her.'

'How could you?' I asked, suddenly furious. This was all too much – the fight and the death and the pain, and now this? Now Cat coming back and seeming so uncaring about it all. About *you*. 'She's so worried! You're letting her worry! It's not *fair*.'

Cat crossed her arms defensively but her eyes were troubled. 'I know, Tess. But if she knew I was still alive, she'd send me right back to Cascade Falls. And I can't just go back there. I was a loser there. I'm not saying I've got it all figured out now but, well, at least there's no Charlotte Lord here. She still rules the school, I bet.'

I nodded. Then another thought struck me. 'Is she one of them? I remember her chasing you. I remember her calling out to her dad that she'd *found* you.'

Cat shook her head. 'I can't be sure, obviously, but I don't think she's in on it. I think she knew her dad needed to find me, and she was helping him, but I don't think she knew *why* he was looking for me. You know this, but you've forgotten: I was in trouble at school that day. It wasn't my fault. It was Laurel and Erin. We were on the bushwalk, and we were practising lighting fires from scratch. I got put in their group because I had no partner, and they cheated and used deodorant or body spray or something. Even though it wasn't my fault, we all got in trouble. Anyway, Lord was on the bushwalk with us. It was some big "tour of the school" thing he was doing, letting everybody see what a great big philanthropist he is. Charlotte and her friends were making fun of me for getting in trouble. I couldn't handle it, so I nicked off. Lord chased after me. Charlotte did, too. I guess she thought I was just going to get in trouble. She's a nightmare. She used to treat me like dirt at school. But I'm pretty sure she's just a bitch, not a Diemen. For one thing, there aren't any female Diemens. They're all men. As far as we know, Diemens have only ever been men. Men of a certain age. Charlotte doesn't fit the Diemen mould. Plus, I used to go to school with her, remember? And I sneaked out a lot. I never once saw her leave campus, and she would've had to. To hunt. Unless she only hunted Cascade girls, in which case there would've been a lot fewer of us. Lord's already taken enough of us, but he's careful. He only takes the bad girls. Like those Scottsdale chicks. Most people at Cascade Falls thought I was just as bad as they were. If you hadn't rescued me from them I would have been next. You saved me.'

'I don't remember that yet,' I admitted, still thinking about Charlotte. Cat might think she wasn't involved in all of this but I wasn't so certain.

'Well, I have to take some of the credit,' said Cat, smiling. 'The Diemens had me. They were running through the forest with me. One of them was holding me by the neck, as if I was a rag doll. I kicked him in the balls and he dropped me and I ran. But the Diemen bastard had ripped a chunk out of my throat. I was all woozy and bleeding everywhere. I reckon I would have passed out, but you burst through the forest and grabbed me. We hid in a burrow for ages until they gave up. You were Thyla and you expected it to freak me out, but it didn't. I loved it. I wanted it. I begged you to change me too. I don't reckon you would've if I hadn't been bleeding everywhere. You thought I was dying. You were probably right. You saved me. You made me this.'

Cat gestured down at her body. At her *Thyla* body. I felt like I was going to faint.

'I did that?' I whispered. 'I *killed* you?'

Cat shook her head. 'You didn't kill me, Tess. You gave me a second chance at life.'

A strong scent filled my nose. Sarco.

I turned around quickly, my heart in my throat.

'Rha,' said Isaac, nodding at the Sarco walking towards us. It sounded like he was talking through clenched teeth. Clenched *fangs*.

'Isaac,' the Sarco echoed, and his voice was just as tense. Having to speak civilly to one another was obviously difficult for them.

I felt my own nose curling. My lip pushing back and my hands tensing. I felt a hundred and sixty years of hatred pulsing through my veins. Instinct was telling me to attack this man, this *Sarco*. The word jangled in my head. Its sound was unpleasant. Its smell was repulsive. I hated Sarcos. I was *meant* to hate Sarcos, though I did not know why.

And yet . . .

I looked across the clearing to where the other Sarcos were standing. I caught Harriet's eye. Her face was blotchy and her eyes were red. Her sun-streaked hair, which I now understood would gradually turn fully Sarco-black as she matured, was messy from having been raked through so often by her trembling hands.

She'd lost two friends. Sara dead. Rhiannah kidnapped. They had been *my* friends, too. They had been so good to me. But they were *Sarcos*.

I didn't know what to think.

Rha ran his hand through his own tar-black hair. 'It's all getting so much worse,' he growled.

Isaac nodded. 'I know, Rha,' he replied. 'I think the time of petty fighting and small battles is over. It's war now.'

'Are we on the same side?' I could see it pained Rha to have to ask the question.

Isaac looked at the ground. 'I think we have to be if we're going to survive. A treaty is our only choice. It won't be easy, though. You know that. You know there are those among us who will not agree to it. Some of them might even actively oppose it.'

'I know. But I think we have to try. I believe he has the poison and is testing it,' said Rha. 'I believe that's why he took Rhiannah instead of killing her.'

Isaac nodded. 'He has the poison, Rha. He calls it the "solution". Tessa heard some of them talking about it before she fell. And tonight one of them whispered to her that Lord has got it working. And there's something else. Tessa saw the Diemens with a Sarco captive. We think it might be Raphael.'

Rha nodded slowly. 'We need your help.'

'You have it,' Isaac grunted.

'We should have done this sooner,' Rha growled. 'One hundred and fifty years sooner. Like you said – petty fighting, small battles. We thought we were doing enough. Why didn't we realise we weren't doing even *nearly* enough? Why did we let it get this far?'

Isaac sighed. He looked out at the clearing. The bodies of Beagle and Sara were nearly gone now, turning to earth and sinking into the ground. I saw his eyes gleam with tears. 'We thought the same, Rha. We thought we had it in hand. I think we just overestimated ourselves. We overestimated our powers – we were here first, after all. We know the land. They're foreigners. We thought they couldn't touch us. I think we overestimated also what we could do alone.'

He said this last part flatly, but still I could sense the pain that saturated every syllable: the pain of losing friends, of knowing it was partly his fault, of having lived so long and seen so much. I could also see it was difficult for him, talking to Rha about these things and admitting he had been wrong.

But Rha had also been wrong. He had made mistakes. And lost friends.

Rha nodded at Isaac and then at me, and moved towards the surviving Sarcos. Perrin looked up as Rha approached.

His black eyes seemed full of fire. His red lips looked soft and pillowy against the strong set of his jaw and his angular cheekbones were even more pronounced in his Sarco form. The scar beneath his eye was still there, and it looked even more dangerous. And attractive.

He was looking at me.

I felt goosebumps rise on my arms.

He was looking at me. And I liked it.

'Whatcha looking at?' Cat asked, breaking the spell. I jerked my head away.

'Nothing,' I snapped, still bristling at the frivolity in her tone. It seemed as though the events of this evening had not affected her at all. 'Just *them*,' I added, realising I may have sounded rude. Perhaps this was how Cat dealt with hardship – by pretending it did not exist.

I sneaked one last look across the clearing. Harriet was looking back at me. 'Goodbye, Tessa,' she mouthed.

I nodded back. My eyes searched for Perrin. He was already gone.

I felt a jolt in my heart.

Cat sighed. 'I know, Tessa. It's tough,' she said. 'They're your friends, but your instinct tells you you're supposed to hate them. Trust me, it never gets easier.'

Isaac, who had moved away to talk to one of the other Thylas, was now walking back towards us. 'Cat. Tessa. We have to go,' he said, abruptly.

'What's up, Isaac?' asked Cat.

'I was talking to Delphi,' he said, gesturing towards a short, stocky female with a shaved head and nose stud. She smiled at me tentatively and I smiled back. I couldn't remember her being there during the fight. 'She was up at Cascade Falls,' Isaac said, confirming my thoughts.

'I was keeping watch,' she said sheepishly. 'I have no idea how they got in.'

'How *who* got in?' I asked.

'A couple of Diemens,' she said, her chin wobbling. She ran her hand nervously over her bald scalp. 'A couple of Diemens got in,' she repeated, 'and they took one. I couldn't stop them. They took a girl. I heard some other girls talking about it. It was during some astronomy lesson. They said they saw her sneak away, heading back towards the dorms. They saw two men, in silver masks, come out from behind the trees . . .'

'Did they say what her name was?' I croaked, a sick feeling twisting my stomach.

'Laurel,' said Delphi. 'Her name was Laurel.'

'No!' I cried. 'Why would they take Laurel?'

Delphi shrugged. 'They knew most of us would be here. I suppose they thought it would be a good opportunity to feed.'

I turned to Isaac. 'Isaac, I need to go to Cascade Falls.'

'There's no point! It's too late,' said Delphi. 'The Diemens are long gone. I tried to track them, but their smell had already faded and that was half an hour ago. Isaac, tell her. We need to get back to camp and –'

I cut her off. 'No, Delphi! I need to go to the school. I know it's too late to find the Diemens, and there's probably nothing I can do at the school either. I just want to be there.'

Isaac nodded. He understood. 'Let's go,' he said.

CHAPTER

thirty-six

WHEN WE GOT BACK TO CASCADE FALLS, YOU WERE ALREADY there. Someone had called you.

Cat had been walking with me, but I felt her pull back when she saw the police car. I turned around to face her. She shook her head. 'I can't do it,' she said. 'I just can't. I can't go back to that life.'

'Maybe you won't have to,' I replied. 'Maybe Connolly will understand. She loves you, you know.'

'I know,' Cat sighed.

'And it's killing her not knowing what's happened to you,' I countered, my voice coming out harsher than I intended.

Tears puddled in Cat's eyes. 'Okay,' she said shakily. 'I'll tell her. I promise. But after this, all right? You go ahead. She needs to do her police stuff. Once it's all over, I'll come out. Okay?'

I nodded. 'Okay.'

When Cat left, disappearing back into the shadows, I turned to Isaac. 'We can't go up there like this,' I whispered, gesturing with my clawed hands at my bent-back legs and my stripes.

He shook his head. 'Of course we can't, Tessa. That's why we have these.' He pulled from his pocket two shiny bangles. 'This one's yours. It snapped on the day of your accident. I only just got it back from the jewellers. Good timing.'

'That's a copper bangle like Rhiannah has,' I stammered.

'It is a *cuff* like Rhiannah has,' said Isaac. 'But it's not copper. It's bronze. An alloy. Made from natural materials, but created by man. It gives us the ability to shift between our natural state and our human one. Without it, there is the risk of us changing at any time, though shifters who have been changed for longer have a higher degree of control. Not at the full moon, though. None of us have control at the full moon without one of these. Here. It's for you.'

He passed me the cuff and I hesitated, remembering the jolt Rhiannah's cuff had given me.

'Don't worry, it won't bite,' said Isaac, laughing.

When I still refused to take it, his forehead creased. 'You've touched one since your accident, haven't you? A Sarco one? Rhiannah's one?'

I nodded. I felt very ashamed.

'Sometimes we put protections on them,' Isaac explained. 'Natural bush magic to make sure nobody takes ours. I reckon that's what Rhiannah did. I can teach you how to do it with yours as well, but trust me, *this* cuff won't hurt you.'

Gingerly, I took the cuff from his fingers. He was right. It just felt like an ordinary bangle. Isaac looked at his with a wry smile. 'It's not part of the official police uniform, so I gotta hide mine. It's more of an *anklet* than a bracelet for me. Very masculine.' He laughed bitterly. 'Now, are you ready to go over?' he asked, gesturing with his head towards Cascade Falls. 'If you're not ready, it's okay. Delphi was right. There is probably nothing we can do. By the time Delphi got back to us, the Diemens would have been long gone. They have probably already –'

'Don't say it!' I cried. I shook my head. 'I know, Isaac. I know Laurel's probably already gone, but I need to be here. I need to make sure the rest of them are okay.'

'You need to protect them,' Isaac said, softly. 'The same old Tessa.'

We began walking towards the school, more slowly now.

Isaac spoke as we walked. 'Do you remember the story of my cuff yet?' he asked. I shook my head. Isaac nodded and went on. 'One night I was walking in the grounds behind the factory, trying to organise my thoughts – I was worried about Hopkins and Chassebury. They seemed to be growing more demented by the day and I didn't know what to do. I heard a noise coming from the forest. It sounded like something whimpering. I followed it and found a creature huddled in the undergrowth. It was a Thyla, half-turned, though I didn't know it then. I was really scared, and was going to run away, but then the creature called out in a human voice. "Help me." The voice was so full of pain, how could I refuse? I moved back over to him and saw that his leg was almost torn right off. He told me that he'd been trying to protect a convict girl who'd strayed too far from the factory grounds when she was collecting firewood. But there had been too many of *them* and he'd lost her, and they'd taken his leg to punish him. Diemens think that sort of thing is funny. I asked the Thyla who *they* were and that's when I first found out about the true extent of Lord's powers. I said we had to stop them. The Thyla, Adam, told me he knew he would not heal quickly enough to survive his injuries but, if I really wanted it, he could turn me so I might have a chance of fighting Chassebury on equal terms. I agreed and he bit me and gave me his cuff. He died soon after.

I wish I could show the world Adam's cuff. I'm so glad to own it. And you won't remember this, but your cuff is special too. We melted it down from a necklace your mother wore. It has the added protection of the love she felt for you. You wear it with pride, okay?'

I nodded, feeling tears well in my eyes. For once, I did not shoo them away. 'Okay,' I whispered.

I pushed the cuff onto my wrist as Isaac clipped his around his ankle.

My muscles turned to jelly. My joints flamed and contracted and shook and burst. My fingers pulsed with pain. My eyes burned. I gasped, and my hands flew to my face. 'It hurts!' I cried. 'It hurts, Isaac!'

'I know,' he said, putting one of his huge hands awkwardly on my shoulder. His hand was trembling. He was hurting too.

'It didn't hurt going the other way,' I moaned. 'Why does it hurt so much going this way?'

'Because "the other way" is your natural state, I guess,' he said, his voice gentle. 'So shifting to that state is kind of like . . . I dunno, putting on your comfiest pair of tracky dacks. Shifting to your human state again is like . . .'

'It's not *like* anything,' I grunted. 'It's agony.'

'Yeah. Trust me. I'm feeling it too,' said Isaac.

'Do you ever get used to it?'

'Tessa, I hate to break it to you, but you've already been doing this for a century and a half, whether you can remember it or not. So no. You never get used to it.'

I began walking again, towards the school.

'Tess, wait,' Isaac called. I stopped and turned. Isaac reached into the pocket of his trousers and pulled out a crumpled t-shirt. In his other hand he held a police shirt – equally creased. 'You might need this,' he said, throwing me the t-shirt. I caught it.

'Thanks, Isaac,' I said, my face burning.

'Don't worry,' said Isaac, walking towards me and punching me on the arm as I pulled the shirt over my head. 'It's nothing I haven't seen before.'

chapter
thirty-seven

WHEN YOU SAW US COMING, YOU BEGAN TO SPRINT towards us, your hand rising up in greeting. 'Vinnie! Tessa!' you called out. When you reached us, you wrapped your arms around me. 'Oh, thank God. Thank *God*, Tessa! I thought I lost you! Vinnie, where did you find her?' you asked, turning to Isaac with your arms still tightly around me. You didn't wait for him to reply. 'What happened to her? Why was she out there?'

'I was out there because I was Thyla,' I said quickly, before Isaac could come up with some lie to deceive you. 'That's what they're called. The creatures in the book. I'm one of them. We both are.'

You gasped, looking up at Isaac. 'What do you mean you *both* are? Tess, really! She's joking, isn't she, Vinnie?'

But something in his expression told you everything you needed to know.

Your face became pale. The freckles seeming to darken, showing like specks of dirt on a marble floor. 'No, hang on. Wait. I . . .' You looked like you wanted to run. Your hands were raised up, and your head was shaking.

'I can't deal with this,' you said. 'It's too much. I . . . I need to go. I need to *think*.'

'Connolly, I'm still the same. We're still the same!' I protested.

I looked quickly at Isaac, afraid of what I would see. I expected him to be angry – his eyes blazing, his jaw grinding. Instead, I was surprised to see that he looked calm, even relieved.

'Rache, nothing has changed,' he said.

The way his voice sounded surprised me almost more than anything I had seen that day.

It was soft. It was kind. It was *tender*.

You still looked as though you wanted to run, your body tilted half away from us.

But you weren't running. You had stopped. You were listening.

'Have you *always* been?' you asked, softly.

'Yeah, for about a hundred and sixty years.'

'Why did you never *tell* me?'

You looked as though you might cry and suddenly I understood the tenderness in Isaac's voice. I'd never noticed it before. But now it was there, painted vividly on the faces of my two friends: in the softness in Isaac's eyes; in the way you were biting your lip, your eyebrows furrowed.

'I never told you because I thought you wouldn't understand.'

'I *don't* understand,' you whispered. 'But maybe I *will*. In time. I'll try. That's all I can promise, Vinnie.'

'Right. Good. Excellent. Well, we'll talk about that later,' he grunted, his voice shifting abruptly to his usual growly tone.

'Where have you been?' you asked again, your voice turning from tender to accusing. 'Where did you take her? Vinnie, what is going on?'

'There are . . . dangers here,' Isaac said, carefully.

'At this school? Has this got something to do with those other missing girls? Because you said that case had been solved and they were safe. And I know that Cat . . . oh, Vinnie! Has this got something to do with Cat?'

'No!' Isaac said, quickly. 'This has nothing to do with Cat. Nothing to do with you. You need to keep away, Rachel. You need to stay *away* from all of this.'

You looked exasperated. 'Vinnie, why on Earth would you let Tessa come to this school, if you knew it would be dangerous for her?'

Isaac cleared his throat. 'Well, Lord wanted Tessa to come here and he's . . . he's such a powerful businessman, Rache. You know that we must be *seen* to be doing what he wants.'

Isaac gave me a meaningful look – a look that said 'don't say a word', and I didn't need to ask why. He was trying to protect you. He was trying to keep you from knowing about Lord because he knew if you did, you'd be in danger. In any case, I felt too nauseated to say anything. I knew Lord had provided the money for me to come to Cascade Falls, but he had *suggested* I come here?

Why?

'And . . . look, Rache,' Isaac went on, 'I *did* know that there were Sarcos here – but they are Sarcos I have come to trust.'

'Sarcos?' you said, wiping a shaky hand over your face, your eyes closing as though you were very tired. 'Vinnie, I don't know what a *Sarco* is.'

Isaac looked at me and then back to you.

'I will explain,' he said, softly. 'I'll explain everything. But not now. All you need to know for now is that the Sarcos were here to protect the girls. And our pack does nightly patrols here for the same reason, as we have done since the school was built. I thought Tess would be safer here than anywhere, with our protection.'

'Okay,' you said. '*Maybe* that's okay. I don't know.'

'It was *necessary*, Rache,' Isaac said. 'Please leave it at that for now, yeah?'

You nodded.

'Now, Rache,' said Isaac, clearing his throat. 'There is something else I need to tell you. Something else happened out there, in the bush . . .'

I heard Isaac tell you about Ms Hindmarsh. I heard the little cry you gave, and saw his hand reach out to touch your shoulder as you struggled against tears. I saw it all, Connolly. But at the same time, it felt as though I was a thousand miles away, and the words were just far-off specks on the horizon.

My body was tired: aching, seizing, shifting and humming. It felt as though all my joints were somehow loose and floppy. Like my limbs were made from porridge.

It felt like my brain was too full of words, memories, ideas and emotions.

Sara was dead.

Ms Hindmarsh was dead.

Mr Beagle was dead.

Rhiannah was gone – *taken*.

I was a shapeshifter. I was immortal. Isaac was immortal.

And Perrin was . . . I could see his face. I *adored* his face. It filled my mind. But he was a *Sarco*.

It was too much. It was –

Blackness hit me like a rock thrown at my head, and I was wrapped in shadows.

chapter
thirty-eight

THE LIGHTS WERE SO BRIGHT THEY WERE LIKE DARKNESS. My eyes watered. It felt as though they were bleeding.

I opened my mouth, and what I wanted to be a scream came out as a whimper.

I pushed my eyes closed again, then opened them immediately. My mind was an even scarier place to be than the outside world.

I remembered.

I remembered *everything*.

I am Tessa. I am a Thyla. I used to be human, a very long time ago. My mother was a prisoner. Her name was Dora Geeves. She was from England. She was transported to Tasmania and imprisoned in the female factory when she was pregnant with me. I lived in the Female Factory most of my life, apart from those few years at boarding school, when I learned to be a lady: a skill I had little use for later in life, but one of which I was intensely proud. After boarding school, the Factory became my world again. I knew how things worked there. I was tough. I was strong. I did not cry. I did not let the Flash Mob see my weakness. They were the mean women, the violent ones, the ones who refused to bow to the system. I admired them, but I hated their cruelty. I would not be like them. I would not become one of the Flash Mob. My mother was not as a strong as I was. She joined them. She said she did it to protect me. I said she was insane. She paid for her decision with her life. The Flash Mob women were the first to go. Lord and his men took them first, because they were the lowest of the low. They were the ones who certainly had no family back home to miss them. They took them and they killed them and they ate their hearts and they bathed in their blood.

I was always rebellious, in my own little way. I'm sorry, Connolly. I know you wished that I would never rebel, but I always have. I could never just sit meekly and watch injustices being committed. And sometimes, I just yearned for some small freedom. I was always safe, though. I knew the boundaries. I was sensible. I often sneaked out of my dormitory at night-time and sat in the moonlight. I liked the moon. I liked the feeling of it on my skin. Later, Isaac would tell me more about the moon: about its cycles; about how I was most powerful when it was full and weakest when it was fingernail thin.

But I knew none of that yet, as I sat in the moonlight in the grounds of the Female Factory. I knew none of that when I saw Isaac change for the first time.

When my mother was taken by Lord's men, I begged Isaac to let me be a shapeshifter too. I knew it was the only way I would be powerful enough to avenge my mother's death. He didn't want to, at first. He wanted me to stay human; to stay *weak* and powerless. He said he would protect me. I wore him down. I begged him. He relented. He saw there would be no other way. And he saw I was strong and determined. He saw I would be a good fighter.

For a hundred and sixty years that flew by as minutes I fought by his side. I lived in the forest, only emerging at night-time to patrol the city. I protected the humans – first the convicts, then the prisoners, then eventually the civilian women.

When Isaac told me it was time for him to join the human world again, as Beagle had, I told him I would stay behind. Keep things running in the bush.

I sometimes fought the Sarcos. They were our natural enemies. They wanted our land. They wanted our food. They wanted to be top of the food chain. It was my instinct to hate them.

I killed a few Sarcos. I killed Rhiannah's kin. But I wouldn't do that any more.

Instead, I would try to help them. I would try to help Rhiannah. She was my enemy, right enough. But she was also my friend and it was my duty and purpose to find her.

I could do it. I was certain. With Isaac's help. With Cat's help. Maybe even with Perrin's help.

I could do it.

I was Tessa. I was strong. I could save Rhiannah.

I needed to start now. I could not simply lie idly in my bed while she was out there. While she was *suffering*. I jerked upwards, ignoring the throbbing, pounding, sickening feeling in my head.

You were there. Looking down at me like you had been the first time. 'How you doin', Tess?' you asked gently.

'Fine,' I said, ignoring the rasp that was scraping in my throat. 'I'm fine. I need to get up. I need to find her. I need to help her. Where's Isaac . . . *Vinnie*? Where's Cat?'

'Cat?' Your face went white. 'What do you mean? My Cat? What do you mean, Tessa?'

My stomach dropped.

When Cat had disappeared into the shadows, she hadn't come back into the light.

I didn't want to lie to you, Connolly. But I did. And, if you ever read this, I'm sorry. I really am.

I looked at you. I thought of how you had done so much to protect me from hurt. I looked into your eyes and I saw they were searching; pleading for some scrap of knowledge about the child you loved so much. I couldn't give it. Your world had been turned upside down today. I couldn't tell you about Cat. I couldn't hurt you more, have you know that she was out there but did not wish you to find her. Instead, I would make her come back to you.

'I didn't mean Cat,' I lied. 'I don't know why I said that. I am woolly headed just now. I meant to ask after Laurel. I wanted to know if you had rescued her from Lord.'

Your brow furrowed. 'What do you mean, Tess?' you said. 'Lord? You mean *Edward* Lord? Tess, Laurel is still missing, I'm sorry. But it has nothing to do with Mr Lord. Why would you say that?'

I remembered the look Isaac had given me; the one that told me to keep Mr Lord's activities secret.

'I'm confused,' I said, feebly. 'I think I hit my head. It's all muddled.'

'Don't give me anything else to worry about!' you snapped, and I noticed for the first time the tension in your jaw and the dark shadows beneath your eyes. 'Sorry,' you said. 'It's just that this is hard for me. I am going to *try* to understand what is happening with you and Vinnie. I can't promise I ever will, completely. But I love you both. So I will try. But all of this – Cynthia and Laurel and Rhiannah going missing – it's a lot to deal with. And that's not even . . . Hell, Tess! You and Vinnie are *werewolves*. Or were-*tigers*. Or whatever. That's *big*, Tess. And on top of all that I feel like Cat is slipping away from me. Like somehow this is all tied together. What happened to those girls – maybe that's what happened to Cat. Something horrible is going on out there in the bush. If Cat was involved in it, then maybe she's gone. For good.'

'She's not,' I blurted. 'I mean, I *believe* she isn't. And I'm going to work to get her back to you. And the others. I'm going to get them back too. I'm going to leave this school and I'm going to go out there and search for them. Every day. Until I find them. They're my responsibility. They're my friends.'

'Tessa, how can you do that?' you sighed. 'You're just a girl.'

'I'm not just a girl,' I protested, my voice rising. 'I'm *Thyla*. I'm powerful. I know things. I can *do* things. I can do this.'

You shook your head. 'No, Tessa. I'm sorry. I know you have this *thing*. This . . . were-*whatever* thing, but you are *still* a little girl. And look, no matter what I say, no matter how hard I am finding all of this, I'm not going to leave you. I'm going to make sure you get the chance at a normal life, away from all this danger. You never got to have a normal life, did you? I want that for you. So you *are* staying at Cascade Falls. You are going to stay here, and you are going to study, and you are going to *let* Charlotte Lord look out for you, and you are going to be safe. Leave the police work up to me and Vinnie, okay?'

What could I say, Connolly? I couldn't argue with you. You were my guardian. You were my saviour. You were all I had.

I remembered what Cat had said: *'If she knew I was still alive, she'd send me right back to Cascade Falls. And I can't just go back there.'*

Cat was gone. And now you were protecting *me*. And so I had to stay here. I had to do it for you.

So I nodded. 'Okay, I'll stay,' I said.

And I will, Connolly. I will stay here. And I will be friends with Charlotte, just as Isaac is friends with her father. I will watch her. I will learn from her. I will find out secrets that will help me find Rhiannah and Laurel.

And then, when the moon is full and Thyla blood is surging in my veins; when my fingers are aching to grow claws; when my legs are yearning to push back, then I will leap the walls, and I will join Isaac and Cat and Perrin, and we will be immortals together, and together we will find my friends. And we will defeat Lord.

'I'll stay,' I said again.

'Good,' you said. You kissed me on the forehead and pushed yourself up from my bed. 'Well, chook, I have to go and be a big, grown-up policewoman now, so I gotta leave you, okay? I've talked to Miss Bloom, and she said you should stay in bed just as long as you need to. Mrs Bush is acting principal . . .' Your voice faltered and I could tell you were thinking of Ms Hindmarsh again. You cleared your throat and smiled, dimly. You were trying to be strong. For me. 'The principal will arrive in the next couple of days, but until then, Mrs Bush said if you need anything, you just sing out, okay? She has organised Charlotte to be your runner if you need anything: food, drinks, Panadol, whatever. So, you're all set. And you just call me whenever you need me, okay?'

I nodded again. 'Okay.'

You smiled and moved towards the door. As you opened it, I saw a shadow moving to one side, a flicker of white-blonde hair.

Charlotte.

My blood froze.

Cat believed she didn't know everything about her father – about the evil he did. I wasn't so sure. Those pale blue eyes of hers seemed to contain so much that was cold and wicked. I could almost believe she knew it all.

But, like Isaac said, sometimes it's good strategy to keep your enemies close.

Just before you left, you turned to me and said, 'Have you been writing all of this down, Tessa?'

'Yes. All of it,' I said.

'Keep it hidden,' you said, your brow furrowing. 'Just for now. For now. I think that would be safer. And . . .' Your eyes drifted to my wrist. 'Vinnie told me about the cuffs. About what they do. About how they let you be *normal*. Please wear it, Tess. All the time. Will you do that, for me?'

I told you I would wear the cuff always. I'm sorry for lying again, Connolly.

'Good. Good, I'm glad,' you said. 'I just want you to be normal. I want you to be happy.'

'I know,' I said. 'Thank you.'

Then you were gone. The door clicked shut behind you, and all that was left was me and silence and a head suddenly full of one hundred and sixty years of memories. It felt as though the memories were a huge jigsaw puzzle. Most of the pieces were in place now. A few more pieces and the picture would be complete.

CHapteR

thirty-nine

ON the moRNING afteR the battLe IN the cLeaRING, Perrin came to visit me. He was dressed in his school uniform. It made him look younger.

I was in my room. I had been given a day off lessons to recover. The school did not know what I was recovering from, but they saw the bruises and gashes (which were healing quickly, as Isaac promised they would, but were still visible). They knew it was something major.

'Five minutes,' said Miss Bloom as she let him in. 'And leave the door open.'

Then she was gone, and Perrin and I were alone, with the air sparking between us.

'Have you remembered?' he asked, without saying hello.

'Some,' I said. 'Most –'

'Have you remembered *us?*' he said, walking towards me, his voice urgent now. 'Little girl, tell me you've remembered us.'

I looked at him with wide eyes, trembling, unable to speak.

Because I did remember.

Stolen moments, longing, his eyes staring into mine like he wanted to see my imaginings.

Hungry kisses.

Me. Perrin.

A Sarco and a Thyla.

Forbidden.

It felt like dreams, like the dreams I'd had when I was still forming a picture of my history. The dreams that were concocted of memories buried deep in my consciousness. But how had I buried Perrin? How had I forgotten this?

And how had he acted as if he had forgotten me?

'Why did you never tell Rhiannah you recognised me?' I asked. 'Why did you never tell her you had seen me in my human form before?'

'I think you know the answer to that, Tess,' he said. 'It would destroy her . . .' He trailed off, and I knew he was thinking of where Rhiannah might be now; wondering if she was already *destroyed*. He shook his head and went on. 'It would destroy everything. This has to be our secret.'

He moved closer to me. 'I remember the first time I saw you in human form. I saw you change. I thought I had never seen anything so beautiful. I still think that.'

Perrin leaned forward.

And then suddenly, as we stole a kiss that felt like our first and our thousandth, I remembered more.

And more.

And my story changed all over again.

acknowledgements

firstly, a huge thanks to the amazing people at Random House – to Zoe for her faith in this project from day one, to Kimberley for her tireless work, vision and wisdom, to Christa for her brilliant cover, and to everyone else there who has helped to make *Thyla* a reality. Thank you to Angelo Loukakis for reading the start of this novel and telling me it had potential. Thank you to my super-agent, Nan Halliday, for her incredible knowledge and faith in me, and for so many other kindnesses she shows me. I would be nowhere without her. Thank you also to my writing group: Tansy, Larissa, Em, Sarah and Tracey, for putting up with me talking about Sarcos and Thylas and Diemens ad nauseum. Thank you to my parents-in-law, Laurel and Craig, for not minding when I disappeared to write (and also for listening to me gabbling about shapeshifters and immortals and such. I promise, your son has not married a nutter). Big thanks to Mephy Danger Gordon for being my muse. Finally, most enormous thanks to my family and my darling Leigh. You are my clan and my everything.

Watch out for

VULPI

The sequel to тнуLа

Coming soon